Praise for
Richard Godwin

"A tense slice of international Noir that oozes atmosphere."

> —**Paul D Brazill,** author of *Guns of Brixton* and *A Case of Noir*

"Once more Richard Godwin proves he is the only worthy successor to Patricia Highsmith. His Novel is a deliciously tantalizing bit of dark psychological thriller that will make you think twice about whom you make friends with while on vacation. You won't want to put this one down for a second."

> —**Vincent Zandri,** NY Times and USA Today best-selling author of *Everything Burns and Moonlight Weeps*

"Richard Godwin does it again! With the adroit skill of a seasoned writer that knows that human decency is just a fragile scab on a wound that harbors a violent world seething in sex, drugs, lust and death.

> —**Lou Boxer,** Founder of *NoirCon*

"Only Godwin. It's a phrase you'll use often when you get acquainted with the sensual and sultry atmosphere of this master storyteller. This is some of his most accessible work, but it's one of his most textured and refined as well. Only Godwin can pull it off every time like that."

> —**Benoît Lelièvre,** *deadendfollies.com*

"Claude meets Maxine knee-deep in the Caribbean and knows he'd do anything to make her his: anything. But keeping her means raising the stakes: cash, guns, gangsters and a return to his bad old habits. Will there be enough of him left to keep her by the time he's through? Godwin makes his Narrative lethally sexy—which makes this story just right."

—**K.A. Laity,** author of *White Rabbit*

"Don Juan meets the Marquis de Sade meets Kafka meets Jim Thompson meets Richard Godwin who gets them all together in one room and they collaborate. It's a brilliant success."

—**Les Edgerton,** author of *The Genuine, Imitation, Plastic Kidnapping, The Bitch, The Rapist* and others

"With extraordinary writing, characterization, and storytelling, Godwin is truly one of our great writers."

—**Luca Veste,** author of *Dead Gone*

Also by
Richard Godwin

Apostle Rising

Mr Glamour

One Lost Summer

Meaningful Conversations

Paranoia And The Destiny Programme

Noir City

ABOUT THE AUTHOR

Richard Godwin is the critically acclaimed author of *Apostle Rising, Mr. Glamour, One Lost Summer, Noir City, Meaningful Conversations, Confessions Of A Hit Man, Paranoia And The Destiny Programme, Wrong Crowd, Savage Highway, Ersatz World, The Pure And The Hated, Disembodied, Buffalo And Sour Mash, Locked In Cages* and *Crystal On Electric Acetate*.

His stories have been published in numerous paying magazines and over 34 anthologies, among them an anthology of his stories, *Piquant: Tales Of The Mustard Man, The Mammoth Book Of Best British Crime* and *The Mammoth Book Of Best British Mystery*, alongside Lee Child.

He was born in London and lectured in English and American literature at the University of London. He also teaches creative writing at University and workshops. You can find out more about him at his website **www.richardgodwin.net**, where you can read a full list of his works, and where you can also read his Chin Wags At The Slaughterhouse, his highly popular and unusual interviews with other authors.

CONFESSIONS OF A GIGOLO

by
RICHARD GODWIN

This paperback edition published in Great Britain in 2018 by
Black Jackal Books, Suite 106, 143 Kingston Road, London SW19 1LJ

ISBN: 978-1-9997858-2-6

Book layout by Guido Henkel
Cover design by Lieu Pham, Covertopia.com

Papers used by Black Jackal Books are natural renewable and recyclable products sourced from well-managed forests and certified in accordance with the rules of the Forest Stewardship Council.

Printed by ImprintDigital.com, Exeter, United Kingdom

For Lau, we paint it black and gold

SEDUCTIVE GARLANDS.

HE WAS A MAN OF ADVENTURE ADEPT AT SEDUCTIONS, AND he seduced hundreds of beautiful women in major cities across Europe, a Romantic adventurer with a killer's instinct.

#

'They all must feel that they are the only one,' he used to say.

He came to them with flowers and garlands, a promise of more. And if the flowers were real there was more reality to his love that the flesh of the women he satiated. He gave exquisite pleasure to them all, reading and knowing their desires. He dwelt in the shadows of their lives, he resurrected them with his hands. He gave them deep ecstasies, a man who seemed to render fantasy flesh, mystery lover, dangerous seducer, body of female desire, the one they all craved with such deep longing that his lovemaking became an addiction to them, as they lay back on the clean sheets of hotels and apartments across Europe. A perfect symmetry of pain existed in his heart as he allowed them to dwell in their silent desires. He would cover their skins with petals, releasing the gentle aromas into their bodies as their still and dreaming desires were sated by his subtle hands. He caressed the surface of their flesh with the sepals of exotic flowers, which aroused them as they lay waiting for him, yielding in their minds to him before their bodies opened.

Paris Tongue existed on the edge of female desire like a hidden fantasy in the hearts of the women whose lives he touched. And one hot and torrid summer when London seemed on fire with sidewalks cracking in an unreal heat, he met Viola Reger. She was starving in her lonely, pointless marriage and Paris tended to her appetite like a master chef. He knew just how to satisfy a hungry appetite.

Paris conducted affairs with the wealthy wives of husbands too distracted to notice, and women were drawn to him like moths to a candle. He knew the exact amount of attention to pay each of his women, and he kept them apart and visited them only in the Secret Hour. This was the time when he made love to them on Egyptian sheets in antique rooms sprinkled with the finest perfumes, in anonymous hotels on long and lustful afternoons, in the lavish apartments of wealthy friends, and occasionally in places of his mistresses' own choosing. They breathed his name at night, when alone, they looked at their sleeping husbands and they wanted Paris inside them. And he worked his way into them like a silkworm and watched them yield the coin of pleasure, uncaring of the dangers their marriages may present. He was the lover they had always desired. Evasive Paris, the only man to them, dwelling in the twilit shadowland between reality and fantasy.

To look at, it was obvious what chars he held. Paris was tanned and athletic and gentle and dangerous. He had that blond fire about him that warmed without burning, and his blue eyes shone with endless sexual ambiguity. Tanned and golden with the physique of model, he dressed exquisitely well and adapted his style to suit the woman at hand. But it was not just his looks that counted for so much in the romances he conducted, one-sided as they were. It was his acute ability to read a woman's mind and mood. He knew them all, all the different kinds of woman. He also gave them what they needed, reading each fluctuation of their mood. He was a great listener and something of street psychologist, a man who had learned young how to hustle and lie fast.

He could read a woman's sexual needs as quickly as he used to pick pocket the tourists who frequented Piccadilly with cameras on their shoulders and maps in their eager hands, seeking out the culture of the old decaying city beneath which the filthy trains rumbled underground.

He was the bastard child of a killer, and he had survived by trading on his looks and sexual knowing. He'd inherited money from a wealthy uncle at an early age when his exotic fragile mother had fled with an Arab prince to settle in Dubai where after several miscarriages she bled to death one day on an ottoman.

Paris had been schooled at the best boarding establishments across the country, passed a cosmopolitan upbringing, and been looked after on holidays by Flamen Grotto, a disinterested guardian who ran a porn empire. He lost his virginity to an actress who'd starred in Flamen's films, sultry full figured Maria Revel. She seduced Paris one day shortly before he left school as he got out of the shower in his room at Flamen's home. Maria was sitting on the bed and gently pulled the towel from him and took him in her mouth. Then she took him inside her.

Afterwards she said to him, 'Paris am I your first woman?'

He looked at her with his intense blue eyes and no sign of embarrassment.

'You are,' he said.

'You've been wasted in those schools.'

'I've decided to leave early.'

She touched his penis.

'With a gift like that you must be generous.'

She climbed on top of him, noticing his ready tumescence.

As she rode him again, she bit her lip and said, 'You were born for this, you know just how to touch me, in ways few men have been able to.'

'It is easy to give and experience pleasure.'

'For you perhaps, do you think I am a whore?'

'What is a whore, a whore can be a man also.'

'We cast aside our morality.'

'They is much hypocrisy and cant surrounding sex, especially where marriage is concerned.'

'Keep pushing, that's it, deep inside bury it in me Paris, so that I may be reborn in ecstasy.'

These were the early lessons that formed a pictorial tableau in his memory later when he would look back at his early days. They existed in lurid technicolour in his mind.

Paris learned from Maria Revel. She taught him how to use his tongue and how to arouse a woman quickly by touch. She brought her niece Sarah to him, a shy virgin whom Paris fucked one night beneath a blue moon. Her pale breasts were filled with moonlight and the veins beneath her alabaster skin stood up as she came, her hips arching and her cries echoing into the stillness of the sleeping gardens that yawned like a lake beyond Flamen's wealthy mansion. There was nothing virginal about her in that moment, because she had wanted this for years and now fantasy became reality.

'You have helped her, her confidence is now sky high,' Maria said, claiming him afterwards and drawing him to bed, where she pulled him deep inside her as he saw jealousy flicker in her eyes.

He made mental notes of these moments of emotional vulnerability in the women he proceeded to bed with great style. He never felt jealousy himself and knew what that represented to the women he encountered. Paris only stayed one more term at the exclusive school. He progressed from Maria to the mothers of school friends whom he seduced with aplomb on afternoons when they were alone. He began with one women he had his eye on for some time, a clearly sexual being who he estimated needed a certain form of excitement.

Karen Flame was a brunette beauty who turned heads every time she visited the school that existed like an artefact on the edge of England, a throwback to a rural past. Paris brought her some flowers and put his hand in her blouse as she made him tea. He heard her gasp before she set her mouth on his and reaching into his trousers took him in her hand.

He undressed her slowly, first unhooking her lace bra and feeling her full breasts with their saucer like nipples. Then he removed her panties and ran his finger inside her waxed cunt and listed to the erotic song of her gasp. His tongue was in her mouth as he aroused her with his finger, and as he looked into her eyes he saw the lust he knew was there. He'd known it when he used to watch her come to the school. Some women sought eternal youth in sex, it was the fountain of Eros. They came to bathe and to be penetrated by sin, and he gave them what they wanted. Karen was not old by any means. Still voluptuous and carnal, still alive and young enough to stir many men's loins, she knew that age was coming. Paris was a doctor. He was a sexual priest who administered youth through sex and he gave her orgasms she had never known before.

She wrapped her toned legs around his neck and pulled his hair as he licked her, issuing a fine spray of come from her perfect, wet, sliced peach.

He licked his lips and looked into her emerald eyes. He could see the million ways that she desired and at the core if it all was the need to be desired. He conjured the illusion of that need and gave it flesh. Actor, lover, erotic habit, pleasure. He was all of these and a man who penetrated to the core of the female mind, because seduction and pleasure were all in the mind first, that us where they originated, in thoughts that need tending, watering with the exotic until the women were ready to experience what they had always desired in secret.

And so he took them to the secret hour and left them tingling with an ecstasy that was as deep as a dream. Paris was as additive as heroin and he filled his women with a craving. It was a craving so intense it hurt. That in itself was an erotic necessity because he knew well the fine, fragile, sensuous, quivering line between pleasure and pain. He worked it like magic.

They called him lover, they called him sex god, they thought of him as a living fantasy, a song, a need, an addiction. They loved him and desired him more and more. His evasiveness tortured and tormented them all. They knew he could never be theirs. But still they persisted in their attentions to snare him to their lives, the one thing that would result in his losing his appeal. They called him slut and brujo, they called him romance, dream, fantasy, ecstasy, pleasure and woman. At times it seemed he was a female in a man's body, but no, he was note of that he was all male, but he knew women through and through. Knew them from their lies to their skins. As he fucked Karen he knew what his calling was in life. He could see it in her eyes.

'You taste like champagne, Mrs Flame.'

'Bring me your hard cock,' she demanded and spread her legs.

Afterwards he looked at her full figure, her smooth skin. He considered her a country, and he thought of Empires, all of them sexual, and the many worlds of pleasure he knew.

'You have a perfect sliced peach,' he said.

'I feel like I'm still coming,' she said.

They lay in the erotic stillness of the house. He ran his hand along the contour of her thigh. He thought of her husband. He would never reach Karen at her erotic core the way he had just now, so easily. That is when it came to him just what he was doing. It was a moral necessity to liberate the sleeping female from the marital shackles and the hypocrisy. That is how marriage seemed to him that afternoon. It was a social chain, and a sexual prison. He decided there and then he would use his inheritance on a life of erotic adventure. He would give women pleasure, seducing them in lavish settings. Each encounter would be different and more extreme in ecstasy. That is what he would do. He would find the sexual core of each city across Europe. Reflected in a city's underbelly, it occurred to Paris, lay the repressed desires of the married. It was not just the married, it was all the morally conditioned women lost in cities locked in heartache. He would free the women with pleasure. It all came to him that day as he fucked Karen deep into the erotic night.

She had her hand on his cock as she said, 'What time is it?'

'It is the Secret Hour.'

And so the time was born. It was a time when Paris would enfold his women with satiation, and a time when events would unfurl at a dramatic pace one boiling London day years later.

For Paris discovered he was a born seducer and he made his way through the world trading in female desire. This scene was but a prelude to a series of dramatic events that resulted from a particular sexual encounter that brought danger to the door and to the doors of his many women, danger that necessary bedfellow of arousal, the needful sense of menace lurking at the threshold of pleasure, its ally and its brother.

His days at Flamen's mansion didn't last long after he left school. The house was filled with semi clad women rehearsing for parts in Flamen's films and Paris would watch them and calculate how many he could have. He enjoyed the full breasted, the lithe and the lean, the olive skinned models, and the young nymphs who bathed in the large bathtub adorned with statues of gods who watched idly as Paris discover his private orgies. He washed them with exotic soaps, noticing the differences between their bodies, and discovering new untold pleasures in the pathways of their available flesh.

He travelled with his inheritance and learned new ways in foreign countries. And he returned to London as a young man with a knowledge of women that set him apart. He knew that most marriages left wives unsatisfied and he decided to be the one to satiate their inner hidden longings.

Paris would visit his mistresses in the Secret Hour. It was a time when they would leave the pain of their lives and disappear into sexual adventure and the gratification of their senses.

He let them become other women in the rooms and apartments he used to seduce them. He would watch them shake off the roles they played as mothers, wives, sisters, daughters and display passions and needs they didn't know existed within them. And he knew how dangerous his gift was, since what he unleashed in his women were all the things the contracts of their marriages held at bay.

He found it particularly interesting to see their own conflict with their bodies after they had exhausted themselves in the enactment of fantasies they'd kept well hidden from themselves. He always let them breathe deep of the perfumes he used to create the atmosphere they needed. The luxuriant flowers, the aroma of sin, the soft music and dimmed lights.

He took them away from their lives and the homes that hurt them and he made them all feel beautiful and exotic. Knowing he catered to fantasy he sometimes wondered if they felt it.

'For woman fantasy is the key part of sex,' he said.

He found the women in every venue and situation. He sought them out in shops and restaurants, in the tired back alleys of small sleepy villages where he could see the loss of hope in their demeanours, in bars where they sat drinking with the look of desperation in their eyes.

He would visit them in different parts of London, a city he felt had many natures like women. London, the erotic city that never slept. London, that seemed to conspire with him in seduction. London, the city that hid his penetrations of his women's bodies with its traffic and noise. Paris thought how as he visited them each seemed to have acquired a flavour of the area where they dwelt, existing on the edge of passion like lips forever parting in the rain.

None of them ever smelled the other women on his skin. He would return to his apartment where they never visited him and shower with oils and apply quantities of a light cologne he used before visiting the next one. He had a scent he wore for each of them, and was an astute judge of the type of aroma they desired to inhale when they were penetrated. He never entertained visitors at his apartment, where he retreated on a daily basis into a solitude that was essentially and erotically replenishing for him dwelling in his Gigolo reality. He chose the scents he wore with care and insight, and they always lingered when he left the women, immersing them in memory and carving.

Paris chose to ignore their other lives, the ones they led in marriages stale with rehearsal. And it was this that led him to a series of events that summer that changed things dramatically and ushered in the danger he knew existed like a shadow at the hem of his liaisons, like a violator's hand raising the hem of his lover's dress, ready with a knife.

Unknown to Paris, Viola's husband, Max Reger, was a gangster. He'd started as a killer and had got away with murders as young man when he enjoyed breaking people's bones in cellars stained with blood. He'd progressed to dealing in arms and ran a tight outfit called The Club. Its members included Knuckles Jim, whose fists were as large as a man's head, Tiger Chains, so named because he liked breaking people's legs with shipping chains, Al the Wire, a feral man with no fat at all on his body, and with muscles that felt like concrete, and Bobby Hatchet, who removed a policeman's legs with his favoured weapon. Of all of them Max was the most dangerous. Together they traded in guns, selling them to London gangs and interested visitors to the city. Max prided himself on selling quality goods.

'I don't want that crap out there that blows a guy's arm off when he fires it, I want my guns on the streets and anyone who fucks with me will find out just how good my bullets are,' he said to Knuckles, who laughed, his shoulders shaking. 'Viola knows I don't fire blanks.'

Max was proud of his beautiful desirable wife, whom he flaunted at parties and watched with scrutiny in case another man made a move on her.

They had two children and he always wondered how she'd kept her figure.

'Not a stretch mark on her,' he told Chains.

PICCCADILLY.

Viola was a woman with a beauty that made her proud and indignant towards the attentions of men she felt were inferior to her.

Paris saw her one day in Swallow Street. The light caught her hair as she wore a floral skirt that showed off the fullness of her figure. Paris approached her with a confidence she had never encountered. And it was this confidence that swayed her to him. He knew how to approach each and every woman he decided to take to his hour. Viola lacked arousal in her life, she had no pleasure in Max, who used her as an object, and as she looked at Paris she knew he could give her what she wanted in bed.

She had long toned legs and full breasts. She had eyes that sparkled and a full, voluptuous mouth.

He caressed her with romance, arousing her hidden desires with his deep insight into the lonely female heart. He bought her a coffee and spoke of his adventures. He listened to her and she left feeling alive in a way she hadn't in years. She met him a week later and he spent a long lazy lunch with her at The Ivy, a respectable place for the seduction of a married woman, and she drank too much wine and fell into his snare.

With Paris the world about her vanished. He took her to an apartment he had nearby in a Piccadilly echoing with activity and she let him remove her clothes, reassured he knew nothing about her and thinking this was happening separate to her life, a sort of erotic dream near the statue of Eros.

She was surprised at her own shyness, since she'd long wanted a lover, and had seen no way of meeting anyone under her husband's watchful eye. Her reserve wore off as Paris touched her and she let her passion mount. His hands on her skin felt like silk and she entered a deep sensual ecstasy that day when the chains of her marriage began to loosen. And she felt afraid, thinking of Max and what he may do. Paris felt no fear, enjoying her, showing her erotic ecstasy, taking her to where she let it all go, savouring the theft of another man's wife.

He enjoyed that, the sense that he was stealing into a marriage like a burglar and taking away the wives of disinterested husbands who didn't have time for their pleasure. He was the one who gave that to them and he did it well. It was a theft, since the wives never belonged to their husbands again after an encounter, even one, with Paris. He stole their hearts as he entered their bodies on the dreaming sheets.

Viola began to despise Max for his cheap impertinent entrances into her body. She craved meat. She would cook steaks, barely touching their red surface to the pan so that as she cut the meat her plate was running with blood. She felt alone and bitter at the isolation the Secret Hour caused within her day to day life. And she slipped fast and without knowing it into the addiction to Paris Tongue that would change her life.

Max would stare at her with incomprehension, seeing the disfiguring of his wife as she wiped the blood from her mouth. He felt the victim of some theft and he searched his house for the ruins of the woman he knew. He scoured her address book in vain for the names of lovers and found nothing, leaving only with a vague sense of guilt and a certainty she was deceiving him. For she never wrote any details down about her encounters with Paris, their sexual exchanges were not documented. But her flesh held a record of them, and her face did, and she was watched and not alone. The idea that she was sleeping around unhinged Max and drove him into violent thoughts. Viola was his and he had never thought this would happen, despite his possessive watchfulness of a woman he considered his property. He had ways of hurting people. He thought of them all each time he suspected Viola of a betrayal that was incalculable to him, an event conjuring dark emotions in his criminal heart. For the first time in his life Max began to feel like an extra in his marriage. He wanted revenge against an unknown target.

Max found Viola with her back turned to him at night beneath sheets he fumbled with to enter her clumsily and leave her staring out of the window searching for Paris's face. For it was the night time that Paris brought to his seductions, filling his women with sexual passion and making them crave the cover of dark for the fulfilment of their secret selves. He knew all too well the price they paid for marriage. Suppression of their identity was what it cost, and he allowed them to be who they really, secretly were. Paris realised all too well that men caused the problem. They needed to tame their wives and when their wives played a role they felt secure. They needed to define their sexuality to allay any sense of threat. The women went along with it for security. But the price was independence. Sexual independence. But deep down these women wanted something else, another life, one filled with appreciation and pleasure. That is what Paris gave to them. He opened them up indie. Sex was a key. It was their hearts he was unlocking in the Secret Hour.

Paris explained to Viola that marriage traded passion for a lie and that sexual freedom existed only in the fleeting encounters they exchanged away from their lives. But Viola was not free in her life, and Max Reger, with his hungry eyes, found out about Paris. Not wishing to involve his gang for fear of ridicule, he hired a man known as Floyd the Lens, who had the ability to find out any sort of information he was commissioned to.

Viola left one morning to meet Paris, travelling by taxi from her house to the hotel where he'd booked a room for their afternoon's love making. And Floyd tailed her in his white van, grinning to himself all the way, knowing how much money Max would pay him for the evidence of his wife's deception. Sometime Floyd would take pictures of wives in sexual encounters, good shots of them naked and alone with lovers who ended up dead. He put the shots in what he considered was his professional portfolio, and showed them to clients.

He watched as Viola got out of the taxi. Paris was waiting for her and together they went into the hotel while Floyd's camera shutter whirred in the stillness of his van. He timed the liaison and watched her leave an hour later. He took the pictures to Max, who sat with his leather sole tapping the ground in his night club office.

'Who is he Floyd?' Max said.

'I don't know.'

'Find out.'

'OK.'

Max slid an envelope across the desk. Floyd counted it outside, a few grand for the pictures.

Max called through one of his waitresses, gave her some money, and watched as she slid out of her skirt. He put his hand on the back of her neck, bent her over, unzipped his fly and entered her from behind, seeing Viola's face grinning at him from her back. He emptied himself inside her, and zipped himself up. But he could not empty himself of his rage. Later that day he used his knuckledusters to beak four bones in the face of a man who owed him some money. As Chains picked the man up from the ground Max still felt rage whipping inside him like the tail of a snake, and he smashed his fist into the man's face. He knew who he wanted to hurt.

All night as he drank vodka at his club he saw the face of the man who was fucking his property.

'You're in a funny mood,' Chains said. 'You normally leave the violence for us these days.'

'Yeah, well, gotta keep your hand in don't you?' Max said, standing up and emptying the bottle of Smirnoff into his glass. 'Or you might end up going soft.'

He thought he would kill his wife's lover and make Viola watch.

Over the next few days Floyd tailed Paris. He found out his address and took it to Max. He also took evidence of Paris's relationships with other women, good pictures of him meeting with them that pleased Max immensely. He stared at the shots feeling he was wining. He looked at Floyd.

'I bet they all got husbands,' Max said.

Floyd nodded.

MAYFAIR.

The day Max followed them Paris met Viola on the edge of Mayfair while London ticked like a clock in the rain. There was a curious tension she felt that day of pleasure and heartache. The sense that time was passing her by. She wanted to shop for perfume and Paris accompanied her as they sheltered from the downpour which was washing off the canopies in a curtain that left deep puddles on the ancient paving stones. As she bent her head to smell a scent the shopkeeper had sprayed onto a piece of card Paris thought how beautiful her face was, and how even more beautiful she was when she came. That was the portal to her heart, the opening to the woman who now craved him more and more.

'My friend has a house near here, a place where we can be alone,' she said.

They lunched at a small bistro, while Max sat in his car, his sweating hand gripping the Glock in his pocket. Viola consumed the better part of a bottle of Dom Perignon. They dined on salmon and cheese and she thought of lying on soft white sheets as Paris entered her beneath London's dreaming skyline. He had made the world real again. And the idea of not having him seemed unreal to her, and more threatening than violence. When she was with Paris her other life did not exist. Each moment with him was entire in itself.

They walked from St Martin in the Fields to Duke Street, followed by Max. Paris touched her in Albemarle Street, and kissed her in Dover Street. They passed the seventeenth century buildings with their dreaming facades, then walked along the areas owned by the Rothschild family and the Crown estates, slices of wealth in the heart of the capital, two lovers lost in an eroticism that placed them beyond the cares of workers in offices in the commercial district. Beyond the hedge funds where millions were made each minute, the real estate businesses where the best competed for a higher rung on the ladder, Paris and Viola filled their day with pleasure.

They shopped at Burlington Arcade, ordered there by Lord George Cavendish, on what had been the side garden of his house, reputedly to stop passers by throwing oyster shells over his wall. Paris bought Viola a cashmere cape from Ana Konder and later that bleeding day ran it across her pert nipples when at twilight he fucked her by an open window in her friend's watched house. She leaned across its sill and stared down at the peopled street below, Paris's cock deep inside her, his balls slapping her tight buttocks, as Max Reger stared in blind fury at the pleasure on her face.

They walked along Berwick Street, pausing to look through the windows of its record shops and fabric shops. Viola was wearing a floral skirt and shapely blouse, a little open at the top and from time to time Paris could see her full cleavage rise and fall with her breath as she spoke to him. They passed the small street market, and walked through the noise and commotion of rapid trading, onto Carnaby Street where they contemplated the nature of fashion and spoke in hushed syllables of what clothes suited women best.

They wandered past Dean Street and the Soho Theatre and stopped at the French House pub to drink more wine. And as they left Paris touched her waist. She thought of his hands wandering across her naked body. Then they walked along Denmark Street and entered Golden Square where Viola turned and said, 'She is away, we can take our time.'

'I always take my time with you.'

'I am a passionate woman, do you know what you have done to me?'

'Made love to you.'

She looked at him and narrowed her eyes and Paris saw something he'd felt in her body when she came alive during sex.

'You have penetrated me to the core,' she said.

She showed him into a large Victorian house, well kept and romantically adorned. Upstairs, he walked across the room and touched her face and she fell into his arms. And he undid her blouse, button by button and took her full breasts in his hands and his mouth, his tongue lapping around the edge of her hard nipples.

She pulled off his shirt and ran her hands across his chest as he slid her skirt down and removed her panties. She took him into the bedroom. Paris watched as she took his cock in her hand. She ran her delicate fingers around the knob as he played with her cunt. She turned and stared at the image in the mirror of Paris naked, erect, touching her breasts and sliding his finger inside her pussy. She ran her slender finger along the shaft and bent and took him deep into her mouth feeling it throb there beneath her wet and salivating tongue.

She lay back and said, 'Enter me.'

And Paris fucked her all that dreaming afternoon until she dissolved and lay there panting, emitting small gasps on the silk sheets next to him as twilight fell beyond the Hornbeam trees on Golden Square.

TWILIGHT ON GOLDEN SQUARE.

OUTSIDE MAX REGER SAT SMILING IN HIS CAR AND MADE A call on his mobile.

'It worked, they think they're safe in there.'

He'd paid the husband of Viola's friend to let her have the house and watched the lovers walk into his trap. He'd waited there so he could catch them in the act.

Now he got out of his Mercedes and wandered across the square with the key to the house in his hand.

Viola was in the shower, reluctantly washing Paris's scent from her body when Max ascended the stairs. Paris heard the noise of footsteps and quickly went into the room off the bedroom where he'd just finished penetrating the gangster's wife. Max stood looking around the room, as Viola came out with a towel around her and screamed. Max advanced on her rapidly.

'Shut up,' Max said, and clamped his hand across her mouth.

Viola lashed out wildly, kicking him in the crutch. Max dropped the gun and doubled to his knees groaning. Viola grabbed the gun from the floor. She pressed it to his head.

'You think you can own me?' she said.

Just then Paris entered the room. He looked at Viola and the husband.

'Viola, please be careful,' he said.

'Be careful? I hate him, I want you my lover.'

'Don't.'

But the shot rang out and Viola sprayed the room with Max's brains.

She ran to Paris and held him in her arms.

'We can be alone together now, make love to me here as he lies there.'

He shook his head.

'I am the man you love during the Secret Hour,' he said.

'Are you rejecting me?'

'I am your fantasy, I can never be part of your reality.'

'I have just killed my husband.'

'Then you are free to pursue your sexual interests.'

'My sexual interests? I want you Paris.'

He held her then and looked at her.

'This will never be. I am something apart, a man who wanders into female dreams.'

'The way you make love to me, we can marry, I am wealthy.'

'You're still wet from your shower,' he said, touching her shoulder.

It was as she was dressing that Paris stole away, and vanished like the long shadows that thinned at the edge of Golden Square in the deep London twilight.

To Viola it was incomprehensible that he was not hers and she sat there looking at the dead body of her husband. Some papers were sticking out of his jacket and she went through them and saw the pictures of Paris with other women.

It was almost dark when a second shot rang out, as Viola placed Max's gun inside her mouth, thinking of Paris's cock there, and blew her life away.

Paris returned to his life of seductions. He sought out more women on the edge of their lives and raised the hems of their dresses, alert to the shadows of their husbands.

NEW FRONTIERS.

AFTER VIOLA SHOT MAX REGER, PARIS TONGUE DECIDED HE would move from London. The sense of her despair lay heavy in the air around the streets where he'd seduced so many women, and he wanted new adventures and to explore new frontiers. It wasn't that her act frightened him, it merely proved to him the thing he'd always known, that he was a romantic proposition who could offer no firm commitments to the enduring things that most women craved, after sex. And perhaps it was this unreachable aspect of his being, he considered, coupled with his looks that made him the living embodiment of female fantasy, the lover who could raise them to the heights of passion, but who may not be there in the morning. Women were contradictions, and he knew how to use those contradictions to seduce. They were all in a state of moral conflict. They wanted adventure and betrayed easily, but they needed someone to shoulder the burden of guilt. He wiped them clean of guilt by offering them an excitement they had never known.

He realised he had no ties, no male friends of any particular note, and this was a product of his calling, the seduction of women. And he considered that the body of woman was a frontier, and that different cultures created new horizons for seduction. He made it his particular ambition to taste the ecstasy of every country's female, to learn the language of their desire. He thought of the women with feigned morals, and the honest whores, the desperate wives, and the lonely virgins, and it occurred to him that a little pleasure was the flavour he could bring to the women he would bed and never marry.

And so he set forth to Paris, the city of decadence and indulgence from which he took his name. He had read how Henry Miller referred to Paris as a whore and he could almost taste her hot flesh as he landed at Orly airport. He wanted to experience her in all her decadence. He wanted to hear her pant beneath him. London was gone, he was in another city and he could almost taste its erotic flavour.

Exotic perfumes rose from the skins of women as he wandered down the Champs Elysees. He noticed their watchful eyes dart in his direction and the demure coy way they had of looking away, and he looked forward to enjoying them. He wondered what frenzies their desire would reach with his hands exploring their bodies.

He immersed himself in crowds, lingered in doorways, and watched the idle wealthy wives shop. He gazed at the designer shops and listened to the women talk, when he would sit at cafes sipping an espresso. He was fluent in French and Italian, a product of his education.

He seemed to acquire the shape and form of cities, as if he was amorphous and dwelt in some land of sexual acquiescence to the things that others desired. He dwelt at the edge of desire. He savoured the sense of fulfilment he gave to the women who came to him hungry and alone. And he elevated their passion to a pitch from which he took the things he needed.

ISABELLE'S SECRET.

On his second day there he met Isabelle, a demure and beautiful divorcee who allowed him to buy her a cognac as restaurant. She had gemlike green eyes that sparkled with sexual desire, a pert mouth that made Paris think of the shape of her vagina, and a nimble toned figure. As she ran her finger around the edge of her glass Paris could tell how she liked to be touched. They sat and talked until midnight about London and the places she had visited.

'What brings you to my city, Paris?' she said.

'I heard the women here are more beautiful than anywhere else.'

'And do you find the observation to be true?'

'I think I have found the most beautiful one of all.'

She spoke of her husband and her desire to travel the world with a man who understood her.

'I have needs that many men are afraid of,' she said.

'And what might they be?' Paris said.

'A woman never tells, you must find me, Paris.'

'I think I already have,' he said, as her hot thigh brushed his leg beneath the table.

They talked into the night. Paris found the key to this woman, there on that first night in Paris.

She sipped her cognac and he watched her moist lips as she said, 'I have a secret, and if you find it you will find me, Paris.'

She laughed and looked away, along the empty streets across which a pink dawn was breaking.

She took him to her apartment, a tidy affair near the Arc de Triomphe. Silks and satins adorned the living room, and Isabelle subdued the lights, her face watchful and hungry in the erotic twilight.

Paris undid her blouse, undoing each button slowly as she began to pant and he ran his hand inside her bra, popping her pert breasts out of her bra and erecting her nipples as she undid his zip. She looked down as she held him in her hand and ran the tip of her tongue across her wet erotic lips.

'Fuck me Paris, I've always wanted to be screwed by my city.'

He unzipped her skirt and she pulled down her panties. She was waxed and her lips were full and shapely, wet and smooth to the touch. He ran his finger inside her.

Isabelle lay back on the bed and he licked her softly, slowly increasing his rhythm as he flicked her twitching clit with the tip of his tongue and she massaged his throbbing cock vigorously, until she met him with a spray of come that left her moaning.

'It sprayed put of your pussy like champagne,' Paris said.

She ran her finger across his cheek and stuck it in her mouth.

'I do taste good,' she said, pulling him towards her.

Paris entered her and fucked her until morning when she fell asleep.

When she awoke she walked naked across the bedroom to where Paris was looking out of the window.

She came over to him and put her hand down his trousers. She pulled his cock out and looked at it.

'Give me more, fill my hole with this huge cock.'

He aroused her with hours of foreplay, and screwed her until she lay panting. He watched her ride his cock like a piston, rising and lowering her wet cunt on her haunches as her nipples stood out on her breasts like bullets.

Finally they went out to eat in the dusk that fell on the erotic streets.

Paris watched the beautiful and decadent women dine. He caught their glances as they looked at his handsome, toned body, his blonde hair, his tanned face and blue eyes. He watched them cross and uncross their legs, many of them without underwear, and fiddle with the collars of their blouses, their breasts rising and falling beneath material he wanted to peel away.

He knew he could cater to them and he could read the manner of their sexual needs in the way they sat and the way they laughed.

He enjoyed the barely disguised sexual nature of the city, its craving for arousal and its steady feeling of erotic display.

He knew the women surrounding him would be easy to seduce at the right times of day and impossible at others, for they all led double lives, and he would penetrate the gap between them. He would part their full thighs and enter them, and leave them dripping on their beds.

He sensed how these Parisian women wanted to be spoken to. Paris knew the things they wanted him to say.

They would never openly admit desire. They feigned disinterest well, but Paris knew what cravings that hid.

#

One day Paris touched Isabelle as they were walking through Pigalle. There, surrounded by whores, she took his hand and lowered it to her cunt, pressing his fingers deep into her hole, through the skirt she wore. She gave him an open look of recognition filled with pleasure. And he knew he had found the key to this Parisian woman.

'I like to be fucked outside, watched by others,' she said.

He took her to a quiet alley behind a restaurant and entered her against the wall.

'You have found me out,' she said.

He fucked Isabelle in more and more daring places. Her need for excitement was an addiction that ran deep in her. One afternoon in the Louvre she sat on his lap as they looked at the smiling face of the Mona Lisa. She was wearing a loose skirt and no panties and she lowered herself onto his pulsing cock, wriggling up and down and biting her lip as a guard looked at them with curiosity. She felt him fill her cunt with hot semen and walked gaily away from the gallery to the Seine, where she said, 'Fuck me from behind.'

Paris raised her skirt and thrust his cock inside her.

'I can feel your balls against my thighs as I look at the Seine, I can hear my buttocks slapping as you pound me with your hard manhood, fill me with come Paris.'

And so he did, among the swarming streets and parks of the city from which he took his name. Until one day a Gendarme saw them and chased after them, catching Isabelle and arresting her.

#

After Isabelle, Paris seduced a woman a week, existing on the money they threw at him. He screwed the young wives of bankers, long into the afternoons. He fucked the older wives of local politicians, who craved his cock and screamed for it while drunk on Pernod. He entered the hot bodies of the university students who wanted long conversations about feminism and hungered for a penetration that troubled their philosophical outlooks. He screwed the waitresses who approached him as he sat eating, and wanted to ride his cock into the night then lie beneath him as he brought them to further orgasms. He bedded the wealthy and the beautiful, he entered them from behind as they stared out of windows and shouted obscenities into the Parisian streets, he bedded them in hotel rooms, sliding his large cock into their dripping cunts.

He wanted to try all the flavours of the Parisian menu. He met the wife of one wealthy Parisian businessman every day for a week at her home where he gave her pleasure. She was middle aged and full of lust. She was buxom and large breasted and she liked to be fucked all day while her husband was at work.

She would say, 'Slap my arse and fuck me.'

And so he would administer slaps to her large buttocks. She would bend over as he did so and play with her cunt. It would drive her into a frenzy and she would pull his erect cock from his trousers and rub it vigorously before sucking it and mounting him. Then she would lie back and he would enter her and watch her scream as she came.

He liked to feel her ample thighs around him as he entered her deeply on slow afternoons when all he heard were her low and rhythmic groans. Sometimes she would shout obscenities as she came and then wander around her house naked sipping wine, touching herself as she spoke to Paris.

Paris learned the city through and through, he knew every taste of it. And the Parisian women began to know of him and his reputation. He found the knowledge unattractive and thought of what he wanted with all these women. He concluded he wanted to understand all aspects of female desire.

He decided he would try different women from the ones who belonged in the city of eternal desire. And so he began to look among the tourists.

UNLOCKING DESIREE.

He met Desiree at a restaurant. And he knew immediately what she was there for and why she had come to Paris, to be desired in the way that would make her alive again.

She was in a way the erotic denouement of his time in the whore city, as he had come to think of Paris. Lost among its fetid streets, its lanes like dripping loins, the facades of its buildings like the naked flesh of a young nymphomaniac, Paris felt he was constantly copulating with the city itself, as if its stones opened up at night and dragged him in towards a pulsing cunt. Behind the glass of every window women seemed to be undressing. And still Paris didn't measure the effect he had on them.

One afternoon he stood in the golden sunlight of Desiree's rented apartment on the second floor of the Boulevard Saint Germain.

He was washing as she watched him from the bed where the sheets lay strewn and she felt lost in him.

He bent and splashed the water on his face in a gesture at once timeless and erotic, made more so by his being watched by her and she fell that day. It was as if someone had opened a trapdoor, which let her tumble headlong into the past beyond her measureless doubt, and she landed in the tanned and muscled arms of her unknowable lover.

He slipped on a pair of faded jeans, his muscles accentuated, and she craved more of him. She thought about his appeal. There was so much about him that set him apart from other men. He had a soft tongue. It wasn't just the way he spoke, his tongue felt softer in her mouth than anything she had ever tasted. It was like he was unlocking her, and showing her the things she'd kept hidden all her married life.

He turned to her and smiled.

'I have to go,' he said and kissed her with the lingering trace of passion that left her hungry and alone.

In the apartment Desiree gazed at herself in the mirror.

'Just another American woman finding her gigolo,' she said, applying her makeup.

She sat alone that lunch time at the small bistro where a businessman glanced at her with disinterest. She thought how her red top stood out among the subtler Parisian fashions. She'd learned French and understood most of the conversation that surrounded her, apart from the heavier argot. And so she listened, trying to be part of the sighing city.

She drank her wine and waited for him to arrive. Desiree had never experienced any man who could make her feel the centre of the world in this way. She pushed her doubt to the edge of the table as he walked in.

It was the enjoyment he offered, the sheer pleasure of his beauty that freed her from herself and she needed him like a drug.

His eyes were like some undiscovered cobalt blue jewel and when he entered her she felt purity.

This grieving widow would never feel alone when she was with him.

He went shopping with her. How to hook this beautiful young man, she asked herself, and took him back to the apartment.

That sunny afternoon she used him in all the ways she'd dreamed about during the years of marriage that had now ended and she felt curiously freed from her grief, as if the rehearsed response she'd known was suddenly removed. She'd done the things she was expected to do when her husband had died, and as Paris slid his cock inside her she realised she had never been made love to all these years. It was the way he entered her, without taking, which allowed her to see that she'd been a prisoner and the sudden death had liberated her.

That afternoon as the golden light streamed through the window and turned to dusk she lost herself and didn't feel the small scar he traced at the edge of her soul with the knowing casualness of a male whore. She didn't feel the bleeding among the rush of fluids in her body and when she went to look at herself in the mirror she thought she looked the way she did before she got married.

They lay and drank red wine and he made love to her again before going out to eat.

And still she hungered for him.

Her legs were weak and she ached and she needed him inside her as he sat there laughing over dinner.

The waiter leant too closely into him and she felt a flash of fury as if she sensed how deceived she was.

And he looked into the heart of her desire without the shadow of a broken promise since all he offered was a necessary illusion.

He took Desiree's arm and led her home.

As she undressed he admired her.

She was a good looking woman who was a few years older than she needed to be to start another life that would fulfil her needs.

She had a full figure, good looks, and yet the skin was beginning to hang beneath her arms and the marks of age were clearly there.

She'd drunk too much and wanted to sleep. The other night she awoke to find he'd gone out.

She came over to him and pulled off her panties, then she bent and unzipped his jeans and put her wet mouth around his cock.

As she sucked him she thought of what her money could do, biting slightly and enjoying the springy sensation of his hard cock in her mouth.

She cupped her hand around his balls.

'I want you to come,' she said.

'I can't.'

'You're hard.'

'Yes, no more spunk tonight, Desiree.'

She stood there looking at his erection and rubbing it.

'OK. Then that's a waste, come fuck me.'

But it was afterwards that she felt angry. She felt as though an unseen hand had slipped a bridle in her mouth.

She lay there and watched him sleep and wondered if he were real.

Once as dawn fell from the sky beyond the Paris rooftops she fetched a razor from her purse and paused before it touched his skin. She felt as though she were about to violate a god and wondered what this made her.

It struck her as comical that she carried this feeble weapon around, as if she needed to defend herself against some unknown assailant. She took some pills and went to sleep.

She dreamed that she was beating her dead husband.

Paris was washing when she awoke.

She got up and walked over to the bathroom.

'My marriage was lonely,' she said. 'My husband went away for weeks at a time. I knew he was seeing women while on business. I turned a blind eye because I didn't love him. I wanted his money. He had this awful way of fucking me, just pushing it in when he was hard. He'd stick his fingers inside me without any feeling whatsoever.'

Paris turned and looked at her. He was drying his hair and water was dripping from his shoulders.

'So Desiree, what are you trying to tell me?'

'That I wish I had found you.'

'You have.'

'Do you know how lonely I felt? Men like him go off on business, fuck other women and return to their wives.'

'Many women feel lonely. You seem sad.'

'I'm grieving.'

'Grief is like the young woman who has just seen how desirable she is, she says she wants you, then she doesn't, she is finding her power. Grief can sometimes be a mask for hatred.'

'Are you saying I hated my husband?'

'No, you are. You say it in the way you touch me and the way you respond when I am inside you, the body does not lie.'

She took his hand and ran it against her cunt and then licked the tips of his fingers.

'Your name means desired,' he said, 'do you not feel desired?

'I do when your cock is inside me, but afterwards my cunt carries the memory of you filling my hole all day.'

They went out to lunch. She had found a new restaurant she wanted to eat in.

Paris was reluctant to go there, saying he didn't like the street, but she insisted.

As they ate in the quiet bistro she became aware that some corner of her soul was torn by the blindness of her life, that her awakening had come too late, and her fate was to be tricked by a whore with the face of a god.

What prompted it was the argument outside.

Two women were having a row and one of them hit the other across the face.

Desiree was trying to tell Paris she wanted more than sex and the noise was causing such a disturbance she got up and asked the women to be quiet.

They looked at one another and laughed.

'This from an old trick,' one of them said.

'What?'

'You sit there with him and tell us to be quiet.'

'You don't know me or my man.'

'Your man. He's no better than a male prostitute, he screws women like you for money, he's a gigolo.'

They walked off laughing, their dispute resolved.

She sat there staring at him.

'They're crazy,' he said.

But there was a flicker in his eyes and she knew.

'Are they?'

'I'm not lying.'

'No, I am. I've been lying to myself ever since my husband died and left me trying to discover who I am when death is standing outside my door.'

She asked to be left alone and paid for lunch and left.

Paris watched her walk away and went to the quarter where he had a small apartment.

He changed and went to the club at the street's end where he seduced a young divorcee.

NEW CITY.

Desiree sat in her apartment considering she should return to America. She slapped herself in the face and screamed 'fool' in the mirror. She went to a hotel nearby and proceeded to get drunk in the bar. She looked at her shoes and her dress and felt out of place among the stylish fashions the other women were wearing. She felt the object of fashionable ridicule and scornful scrutiny. She thought of Paris and his body and remembered the first time he entered her. And she saw a man enter the bar and sit alone thumbing a map. He was obviously a tourist.

She went over to him and said, 'Mind if I join you?'

'Is that an American accent I hear?' he said.

'It is.'

She smiled and slid onto the stool and they talked about Paris and why they were there. And it seemed to her she had found her location in the man whose flesh she craved and he had deserted her because her illusion was broken by the shallow laughter of two whores. But Paris wasn't there, just this tourist.

And at the end of the evening she went up to his room and watched as he staggered around in the twilight, pulling off his clothes.

She thought that the barman had short-changed her and she checked her purse, then remembered he had paid for the drinks. Suddenly she felt cheap and lonely.

She stripped and stood there looking at him, wondering how she had ended up there with him. He touched her and said, 'Come on'.

She thought of how Paris had felt.

She lay down next to him but when he started to climb on top of her she pushed him away and got off the bed.

'Hey wait a minute, you fucking prick teaser,' he said, grabbing her hand.

She was fumbling in her purse as she pulled away, but all she could find was the razor and he lunged at her and she cut him.

There was something strangely erotic in the way his flesh popped open and spurted her with blood and she wondered what it was. She kept cutting him until she sat panting on the edge of the bed.

She felt wet with the juices of death and desire and she thought about her young lover.

She sat there until the police took her away.

As she was driven off by them Paris found another woman.

He walked her to her hotel in the moonlight thinking of the parts of Paris they would avoid.

After he had made love to her this woman looked like so many of the others. He watched her as she lay there sleeping, her breasts pointing upwards from her body. Her cunt looked like a blur in the twilight. Paris looked at the rooftops from the window and felt he needed a new city. He felt the frenzy of Rome calling to him and he wanted to taste the sultry flesh of an Italian woman.

SEDUCED.

The journey to Rome was simple enough. Paris met a young woman named Flora on the plane. He was aware that she kept darting glances in his direction and after a glass of wine, he decided he would talk to her.

She was a Swiss student travelling to Rome to study its history. She wore a tight blue blouse and short skirt and her legs looked long and tanned beneath the sheer tights that hugged her skin. When she spoke she parted her lips in a manner Paris found quite sexually provocative, as if she used a subtext that whispered, 'fuck me if your cock is hard enough to make my pussy come.' He imagined her to have a tight cunt that smelt faintly of the sea air when she was aroused and he could tell what sounds she made when pleasure drove her to the point of agony. As she leaned forward to pour her glass of Campari, he looked at her fingers. They were the sensuous fingers of woman who liked to touch herself and who had not yet been fucked the way she secretly desired. And so he decided to taste her flesh among the timeless ruins of Rome, as if she beckoned him to some deep feminine mystery that never faded.

'The wine is not bad,' he said.

'Excuse me?'

She touched her neck with the demure response of a woman who was now pretending not to have noticed him.

'Forgive me, I felt I was in the presence of a fellow wine lover, it is ultimately discourteous to interrupt the privacy of a fellow traveller, although conversation can help pass the time.'

She smiled then. She had a row of perfectly white teeth and Paris imagined her lips on the end of his cock, her tongue licking it.

'I agree.'

'About the wine or the conversation?'

'About both.'

'Then allow me to introduce myself, my name is Paris.'

He held out his hand and she shook it. In her eyes there was the instant revelation of her sexual desire for him, that moment when he saw a flicker of conscious acknowledgement of the physical fact that beneath the polite mannerisms and the correct words she knew deep down the body was the thing we all held on to, and as time eroded it we craved the touch of the hand that made us alive, the feel of a tongue like silk caressing a woman's clit, or a woman's mouth closing around a man's penis. Although she was young, mid-twenties, Paris estimated, he knew that she worshiped at the temple of sexual ecstasy. The pursuit of orgasms was the secret religion of man and womankind, prelapsarian Adam and Eve naked and lustful, fucking until they dripped in the Garden of Eden. For Paris knew that the return to original innocence was not bound up in moral codes, but knowledge of the body and pleasure. Paris caught a glimpse of his face in the plane's window, and it seemed haloed with promise, the fulfilment of woman's untouched body, the hidden one he reached and tended to like the saint of pleasure, the priapic priest of ecstasy to whose charms all women fell. And he knew how he would take her to bed that night and what he would do to her on the sheets of some Roman hotel as erotic midnight enjoyed its own dreaming ecstasies.

All of this happened in a few seconds as Paris looked at the face of this woman and began to penetrate her mind.

'I cannot match that,' she said. 'My name is far less exotic.'

'How do you like to be called?'

'Well, I am called Flora.'

'And what brought you to France?' Paris said, his eyes lingering on hers.

'My boyfriend.'

'He isn't coming with you?'

'It didn't work out.'

She sipped her Campari and waited for him to continue. Paris knew to let the moment linger while he ran his eyes down her body as she refilled her glass.

She was blonde, attractive, with a toned figure and full breasts. Paris imagined her lying naked beneath him. And as he looked at her he forgot Paris, the whore city. For he was now going to enter the body of his ancient mistress, as he fondly thought of her. And so they talked, of Flora's life, her upbringing in Switzerland by strict parents that, in Paris's view always bred women with passionate natures who secretly considered themselves whores and became the slaves of guilt in later life. Her eyes glowed as she spoke and Paris held them with the image of his cock thrusting deep inside her as he engaged her in the things that clearly mattered to her mind. But it was her body that mattered most and he knew the way to unlock the hidden things that Flora desired.

Soon the plane touched down at Leonardo da Vinci airport. Paris helped Flora with her luggage and as she thanked him she spoke with such familiarity, he knew he had secured her interests for at least a night. It was a night which he would mark with a Bacchanalian ecstasy filled with wine and passion, his entrance to the place where he planned to engage in his most ambitious seductions yet.

'Where are you staying?' he said.

'I thought I'd just find a hotel.'

'Why don't we find one together?'

And so they set off in a taxi and took two adjoining rooms, unnecessarily Paris thought, at Giulio Cesare and met an hour later in the bar. Flora had changed into a low cut red dress, and high heels. As she sat down the contour of her buttocks was clearly outlined by the material of her dress. She wasn't wearing any panties, or was clad in only a G-string, that Paris imagined getting wet with drops of her cunt juice. He imagined taking her from behind as he fondled her tits and she reached under her cunt to feel the fullness of his balls. And so at the bar, entering Flora's lustful mind, Paris gave her the attention of the mysterious, attentive lover every woman dreams of. Paris could smell perfume rising from her skin as she sipped a cool Pinot Grigio, and as he talked he touched her in the dark without his hands, without any physical contact at all, but with the tone he used and the way he looked at her, and he could smell her opening like a flower.

'There are so many places I want to see while I am here,' she said, 'it would be good to have a companion.'

'Consider me yours for as long as you require me.'

There was little wavering in her evident interest in him, and she held his gaze, looking deeply into his blue eyes as they drank and spoke of the places they had visited.

'My family think I am being absurd,' she said, adjusting her shoe. Paris watched her full cleavage rise and fall within her dress, and he imagined her nipples beneath the line of her bra, peachy and erect as he took them in his mouth.

'Why?'

'Because my father is wealthy and believes I should be married and living in Switzerland.'

'And instead you want to travel.'

'I sometimes wonder if I am running away.'

'If a women feels limited she may well do that, chastity belts, after all, belong to the Middle Ages.'

This produced a wave of laughter from her. There was pleasure and arousal in the sound.

They ate at the hotel, sharing seafood, and afterwards returned to his room for a night cap. Flora was standing at the window looking out at the skyline of the ancient city as Paris said, 'You can feel the passion can't you? The sense of time, of how little has changed here. Among the ruins and the newer buildings the same forces exist that helped build the Roman Empire.'

She sipped her cognac and said, 'Passion, yes, that is the feeling, I like that. I think you are a passionate man, am I right?'

'You are.'

'Paris, you have an unusual name and even more unusual manner, you seem to have stepped straight from the pages of a love story with your dashing looks. Oh, listen to me, I have drunk too much. I have talked all night about me and what I want to do and I don't know anything about you. What is it you do?'

'I will show you. I think physical acts are often more expressive than words.'

He crossed the few feet between them and taking her glass from her, set it down on a marble tale. Then he touched her arm, slowly running his hand down to her waist. He slid it around to her back and then Paris unzipped her dress as he kissed her gently on the lips. She was standing there in her red G-string and lace bra with her lips parted in the erotic way she had shaped them when she first spoke to him on the plane. Paris unhooked her bra and touched her full breasts. He kissed her pink nipples and watched them rise. Flora was alive with passion in the hot night. Paris's cock swelled in his trousers and she ran her finger along its throbbing shaft as he kissed her fully on the mouth. She half closed her eyes and he knew what she was imagining. He was a sexual mind reader.

'I'm dripping wet,' she said.

Then she unzipped him and slowly lowered his trousers and jockeys.

'Oh, such a nice generous prick you have, I want to feel it inside me already,' she said, 'but first I want to eat it, I want to suck on it until you are begging to fuck me, my pussy is sweet and hot. How hard you are, do you like it like this, me rubbing your big hard cock? I can see your balls are full of come and I want to drink every drop of it with my thirsty pussy.'

Paris watched her bend and take it hungrily in her mouth, nibbling the end. She looked up at him and her eyes were full of lust, her face flushed in the deep midnight air that smelt of cognac and desire. She moved her lips slowly up and down along the shaft of his cock, sucking and lapping it with the tip of her tongue. Then Paris removed her G-string slowly, peeling it off her body to reveal her beautiful, waxed cunt. He stopped to admire her body, her tight toned buttocks, her full wet lips, then he led her to the bed. He spread her legs and put his finger inside her.

She gasped.

'I told you I was wet,' she said.

'Allow me to introduce you to my second name,' he said. 'He will fill your cunt with a drug that you will crave again and again.'

And so he introduced her to his tongue, parting her lips, kissing each one, and lapping at her clit as he rubbed her nipples. He put his finder deep inside her and massaged her G spot and he licked her clit with the tip of his tongue. He finger and pulled on both nipples.

Flora began to moan, it was a sound full of desire. Paris reached inside her with his tongue, rolling it over her clit as she arched her back. Eventually she pulled him on top of her.

'Fuck me Paris, make me come.'

'That is my intention Flora.'

He pushed his cock inch by throbbing electric inch inside her. And he fucked her slowly, gently, and hard and long, taking her to the liquid place where she began to lose awareness of where and who she was. She was moaning into the night. When she rose from the tangled bed sheets, her thighs were smooth and slick with come as she sipped some chilled Gavi from the mini bar. Then she took his cock in her mouth again and said, 'I want to come so much and so often I ache with arousal.'

Paris slid his hard cock inside her again and unleashed an orgasm so momentous she tore the pillow with her teeth to stop herself screaming.

They slept amid the sound of motorbikes outside and as dawn broke she reached out for him. He entered her wet twitching cunt again until she was flushed with pleasure. In the morning they rose and showered, Flora rubbed Paris's cock with soap as suds fell from her breasts. Then they went out to explore the city, two midnight lovers with pleasure inside them.

#

Paris and Flora fucked and toured. Each night she would wear a different outfit, often with no panties when they went out to eat. She spoke about the things she liked to do in bed. She told him she liked to come in public.

'I used to masturbate on the bus when I first went to university. I was still a virgin.'

'That surprises me.'

'My father was so strict, I was obsessed by sex, but did not lose my virginity until a few weeks into my semester there. The young man was useless, pathetic, and couldn't give me what I wanted and so for a while I slept with women, but I wanted a cock inside me.'

'Were you never detected playing with yourself in public?'

'I sat like this,' she said, moving forward in the chair and placing her hands in her lap. 'My bag of books like so, and I would slip my fingers beneath my dress like so.'

They were in the hotel room they now shared and Paris watched her part her legs and put her finger inside her cunt. She continued rubbing for a while, stroking her clit, watching him as he followed the motion of her fingers, looking to see if there was a bulge in his trousers, then she stopped and licked her finger.

'What did you think about when you used to play with your pussy?'

She laughed.

'Cocks, hundreds of them. I used to watch the men's changing room at university through a hole in the wall with a friend. I was fascinated with them, because my father was so strict. I loved to see the different sizes, some so tiny I wondered if they could give a woman any pleasure at all.'

'And then you lost your virginity.'

'Yes, I met another man, an incorrigible whore he was, and so I didn't sleep with him right away. I used to masturbate him. I loved doing that. I used to take his penis out at the end of an evening and rub it as she tried to touch my breasts and I said, 'No, I am playing with your cock and you will have to wait if you want to fuck my sweet pussy.' The first time I saw spunk shoot out of it I almost came, I was admittedly touching myself at the time, rubbing my clit as he looked at my cunt with his mouth open, almost drooling to stick his cock inside me.'

That night when they went out to eat Paris fingered Flora beneath table of a restaurant and watched her bite hard down on a chunky sausage, so that the meat split the skin in a gastronomic ejaculation as she came, dripping the flavoursome juice of her cunt onto his hand. Back at the hotel she stripped as they entered the room and said, 'Now fuck me with your big hard cock.'

She was still wet and Paris lapped her pussy until she pulled him inside her, wrapping her legs around him. Then she got on top of him and sank her cunt down over his cock so that it was buried deep inside her and she rode him, raising and lowering herself on her haunches as he breasts swung. Paris ran his hand along her tight buttocks and put his finger in her arse and Flora screamed with ecstasy in the swollen erotic night.

'Give me your spunk, shoot it hard and hot inside my cunt, Paris,' she screamed.

RICHARD GODWIN

Next door an ageing couple remembered days on a beach when they explored their passions and the sound of a vibrator started up, deafened by Flora's violent pleasure.

AROUSED.

IT WAS SOME DAYS LATER THAT PARIS WAS OUT ON HIS OWN. Flora had business to attend to regarding her studies and he wandered the city, losing himself among the alleys and bars as he watched the Italian woman coming and going, and studied the nature of their sexual desire.

He was sitting outside a trattoria enjoying a glass of cool Frascati, wearing a light pair of deep blue summer trousers and a white shirt open at the neck when he saw her. A Mercedes stopped directly opposite him, the back door nearest the street swung open, and she stepped out and walked towards him. She was wearing a tight black skirt and deep violet blouse, her face was perhaps the most beautiful Paris had seen, proportionate, yet full of expression. Her eyes were hidden by her sunglasses, and her glowing black hair caressed her shoulders. The skirt hugged her thighs, showing them in the bright sunlight to be full and toned. She walked towards the café in black stilettos and Paris could tell she glanced in his direction beneath her shades. An intense smell of the most exotic perfume lingered in the air after her, but to Paris she smelt of sexual hunger and danger.

He drank his wine and after a few minutes went inside to settle his bill and see if the woman was there. The owner, a fat bored-looking man was going through some receipts and she was standing next to him with her hands on her hips as Paris came up behind her. She had removed her sunglasses but her face was turned away from Paris. He could make out the shape of her pert buttocks beneath her skirt, and the hint of a bra strap running along what looked to be a well-shaped back.

'Can you find it?' she said to the owner, who sighed.

'It must be here somewhere.'

'My husband wants it, he doesn't believe I was eating here two nights ago.'

'I can tell him, you know I always do as you wish, you are my friend.'

'He is suspicious, he wants the proof.'

'Ah, here it is.'

He handed her the receipt and looked up at Paris.

'Sir?'

'I apologise for interrupting the lady, I wanted to pay for my wine.'

She turned then and Paris looked into her deep blue eyes that were set like sapphires in her olive skin.

'You are not interrupting,' she said. 'What accent is that?'

'I am from England, originally, although my ancestry is something of a mystery, a long and tedious story.'

'English? You do not seem English,' she said.

'People usually say that after I am introduced to them.'

'Oh?'

'Because of my name.'

'And what is it?'

'Paris Tongue.'

'Well Mr Tongue what are you doing in Rome?'

'I wanted to visit the ancient city, I want to taste the life lived her.'

'Then you must see the real Rome.'

'I think I am beginning to. May I ask your name?'

'Francesca Agostino.'

He shook her hand. Her skin was smooth and her eyes sparkled with interest as she looked at him.

'Can you advise where to find the real Rome?' he said.

There was a moment's hesitation, a flickering pretence at modesty before she said,

'I run my own travel agency, I can show you.'

#

Paris met Flora for dinner that night and listened to her talk of her day at the college.

'I came here to study history and instead I have been studying how to come,' she said, 'and now college bores me, sitting there while I could be having my cunt stuffed full of your cock and come.'

She bit the tip off a plump fat asparagus, wiping the butter from her lips with a napkin.

'So what will you do?' Paris said.

'I'll continue and we can spend the evenings together.'

'Then work hard and study hard and we will enjoy each other's bodies each night, although I may have some business to attend to.'

'Oh?'

'I am thinking of investing some money here.'

Flora picked up another piece of asparagus and dangled it in front of her.

'Well so long as it's not the business of another woman's snatch. Most men are like this after a fuck, limp, see? I bite the end and the root is hard, but your cock has the staying power of a fortress, it withstands all my volcanic coming, and I want it thrusting inside me every night bringing me to orgasm if I am to study the next day or I can't get the image of your erections out of my head. I sat by the Tivoli fountains today at lunch time and the gushing water reminded me of your cock pumping me with come.'

They returned to their hotel room and Flora took off her blouse.

'Talking of your hard cock, I don't want other women sucking the come from your full balls, ride my pussy now.'

She unzipped his flies and pulled out his penis, and watched it swell with her touch, then she bent and sucked it.

Paris pulled her large breasts over the top of her black bra and sucked her nipples, then he pulled down her skirt.

'No panties, your cunt is wet Flora.'

'Time for a good fucking.'

She got on top of him on the bed and lowered herself onto his cock. She rode it like a piston, her thighs wet, her nipples hard. She pounded him furiously, her breasts swinging, her thighs slapping his balls, and she gasped as his cock filled her cunt with its throbbing hardness. When she came she screamed so loud that a waiter in the corridor paused momentarily with a tray of coffee, then shook his head, laughed, and walked away.

Paris poured them some Cesanese and she lay there playing with his erect cock. Then he parted her thighs and licked her again, tasting her come as he flicked her clit with the tip of his ever attentive tongue.

'Fuck me!' she screamed, 'Pump it deep ad hard inside my throbbing snatch, I am on fire for your cock.'

'I always oblige your erotic requests,' Paris said, 'how could I not my sexually delirious Flora.'

He entered her and pounded her wet pussy until she dissolved, the sheets soaked with her love juices, and she lay panting, her cunt pink and glistening with pleasure.

EROTIC NIGHT.

IT WAS CLEAR TO PARIS THAT FRANCESCA WANTED A SEXUAL adventure outside the confines of her marriage. He met her for lunch two days after his encounter with her at the trattoria, and they dined at Felice. Francesca wore a pink blouse open to her ample cleavage and a tight white skirt that showed her arse beautifully as she walked in high heels. Paris wanted to reach up her skirt and touch the wetness of her pussy as she talked of her city.

'I grew up here, it is my home, although my husband insists on taking me to Naples all the time.'

She emphasized the word *insists* and popped a large green olive in her erotic mouth as she did so. Paris looked at her lips and imagined the lips of her cunt. He pictured her as having a small trimmed dark bush there, and he imagined drops of her cum hanging onto her pubic hair and the noise she made when she entered her orgasms. He could tell Francesca had deep orgasms and that she enjoyed her body.

They ate Baccala al Forno con Pomodoro and Pasta e Ceci o Pasta in brodo di Arzilla, and they naturally and casually shared from each other's plates, as if a form of immediate acknowledgement of the desire that lay between them were there, established by the force and passion of the city that throbbed outside like a violent erection.

'You run a travel agency,' Paris said, watching the way she chewed, lingering over every flavour.

'I have set it up recently, much to the annoyance of my overbearing husband, but I like my independence.'

'Do you give guided tours?

'I plan to, I want people to see the Rome hidden behind the tourist guides, and you can be my first tour.'

'I must say that is extremely pleasant but I do not want the pleasure to be all mine.'

'I do not usually do this,' Francesca said, 'have dinner with strangers, but I feel I know you.'

'You are a most charming chaperone for a man to have.'

'A chaperone ensures propriety.'

'Your husband is a lucky man.'

'Hah. Him, fat pig. He doesn't appreciate me, he bought me.'

'Are you so easily bought?'

'No, I am expensive. I need things he cannot give me and I am going crazy there drinking every night, lying awake listening to him snore and fart.'

Paris filled her glass with Valpolicella.

'Are you trying to get me drunk, Mr Tongue?'

'Would that be such a crime? You are safe with me.'

She leaned towards him.

'But maybe I do not want to be safe, maybe I want danger and adventure in my life.'

After eating they walked through the ancient city, its walls looked golden. And Paris saw desire in Francesca's eyes.

'Is Rome where you grew up?' he said.

'It is. My story is that my father discovered I was pregnant at sixteen. He made me get rid of it and I met Luigi, my husband. But I never loved him. I married him because he was a more powerful man than my father who saw him as respectable. I hate my marriage. Luigi uses me, he is simply a money maker. And I have to go to Naples.'

'Is it so bad there?'

'It is not Rome.'

'What happened to your father?

'He died many years ago.'

'And does your husband know how you feel?'

'He knows nothing, Paris.'

He didn't fuck her that night. He said goodbye to her outside his hotel and arranged to meet her to go on a tour of Rome the next day.

He returned late to the hotel to find Flora sitting naked in a chair.

She rose and ran across the room to him when he came in and jumping up, so he caught her legs, said, 'I have been waiting all evening for you, where have you been?'

'I have met a businessman and am about to make a significant purchase.'

'Stick your cock inside me or I won't be able to sleep, I am tired of playing with myself as I stare out of the window looking for you outside.'

#

It was in the 90s when Paris met Francesca the next day at her apartment. She came out into the street wearing a light blue dress and as she got into her Mercedes Paris caught a glimpse of the gap between her thighs in the bright sunlight. He wanted her all that day as the heat built and they toured the ruins of the city that refused to yield to time. He listened to her narrate the experiences she had there as a young woman, and the many men she had enjoyed and spoke about unashamedly and with an abandon that made him desire her even more.

At lunchtime the shared a bottle of Gavi at a small trattoria and ate Fettuccine Alfredo and Rigatoni con la Pajata. They dipped their forks into one another's plates and Paris saw beneath the gesture the real dipping she desired, the one beneath the politely laid table cloth. As she looked at him she bore the mischievous expression of a woman who was fingering herself under the table throughout lunch. They sucked the fettuccine from their forks, their mouths wet with the sauce.

'You know, Pajata is the intensities of an unweaned calf fed only on its mother's milk,' Francesca said.

'That is why it tastes so good.'

'I sometimes wonder what having my breasts full of milk would feel like, of giving it to my baby. I have not had children and do not want to.'

'I imagine there is satisfaction in the act.'

'Ah, but I want more than that.'

'I know you do, Francesca, I can tell.'

'How?'

'By the shape of your lips and the sparkle in your eyes.'

They returned to her apartment that was packed with antiques, and there among the many rooms Paris fucked Francesca into the pulsing liquid night.

She was pouring Prosecco when he first touched her bare shoulders, running his hand across the nape of her neck. She turned and kissed him passionately on the mouth, exploring it with her tongue as he unbuttoned her blouse. He kissed her brown shoulders as she bent head back, then he kissed her neck and ran his tongue down to the top of her cleavage. Francesca unhooked her blue bra. Her breasts were large and full with saucer-like nipples that instantly responded to his fingers as she reached for his cock and felt its hardness in his trousers.

'So big, mm, let me see your manhood before you take me,' she said.

She slowly unzipped his fly, reached her hand inside, and pulled it out. She looked at it, then ran her finer along the shaft.

'This will make me come,' she said. 'I am going to suck all the come from your cock.'

She began to take off his shirt as Paris removed her dress from her body. She was wearing cami knickers and he put his hand inside them and felt her wet cunt, then he lowered them to reveal the tuft of black hair perched above the most enticing cunt. Her lips were wet and as Paris slid his finger inside her she gasped. He rubbed her clit and admired the glistening oyster between her legs.

Francesca began to rub his cock. Paris watched her take it in her mouth as she flicked its tip with her tongue.

Then she pulled him by the hand to the bed, where she lay down and he parted her thighs. There on the silk sheets he licked her cunt with a steadily increasing rhythm, rubbing her clit, until she sprayed his face with come. It shot out of her lips like a fountain.

'I can spray it like a bottle of champagne from my pussy,' she said.

'It tastes like wine.'

Paris entered her with his throbbing cock. He fucked her for an hour until his cock exploded, pouring hot come inside her wet cunt.

'More Prosecco, and I want you to fuck me by the window,' she said.

She poured them a glass each and they drank, then she rubbed his cock until it was stiff and walked over to the open window that looked down on the Piazza Venezia. Francesca placed her hands on the window sill and looked out into the night. Her buttocks were tight and full and Paris looked between her parted legs at her lips. He slid his cock inside her and took her breasts in his hands and fucked her hard. She arched her back as she came.

'Fill me with come,' she shouted.

And Paris pumped her cunt full with it while below them two young lovers stared up at the source of noise and wandered off into the night giggling.

Afterwards they lay on the bed.

'I have come more times than I can count tonight and I still want you, what is that?' she said.

'It is a desire that only I can satisfy.'

'Such a soft tongue and such a hard cock,' she said. 'And when you ejaculate it sings inside me.'

They toured Rome by day, fucking at her apartment, while Flora studied and waited for Paris each night. Once on a summer's night he fucked Francesca in the back seat of her Mercedes. She sat there with her legs spread and her pussy wet against the leather and Paris entered her cunt beneath a moonlit sky and she dragged her nails down his back as she bit her lower lip and came.

He licked the blood from her mouth.

'I did it to stop myself screaming with passion,' she said. 'The more you put your cock inside me the more I want it, I constantly want to feel it throb and pump me with come.'

She particularly liked being licked before he entered her. Later that night in her apartment above the noise of motorbikes, in front of an antique mirror decorated with gold, Francesca sat on Paris's face, lowering her cunt onto his erect tongue slowly. He looked up at her tight buttocks and the sliced peach between her legs nestled there amid the fuzz of hair and began to lick her cunt until she was screaming, her breasts pressed against the mirror as she hugged it and pushed down onto his mouth. He tasted the glory of her dripping cunt as she showered him with the champagne of her pussy, counting four spurts one after the other.

They seemed addicted to one another's bodies, exploring and tasting their way to new heights. They fucked for days, their bodies tingling with desire. And Flora became jealous and suspicious. Paris had to explain his movements to her, a habit he found tiresome. But when he spoke to her with his cock he silenced her.

FRANCESCA'S HUSBAND.

Paris and Francesca spoke with their bodies. They fucked at every opportunity, at times enjoying each other every hour. They talked of how they wanted more of each other. They talked only of their sexual adventure. Paris sensed another side to Francesca's life, but he didn't ask her about it. He wondered where her money came from and attributed it to her being the plaything of a disinterested wealthy husband.

One day he went to her apartment to find Francesca dressed in thigh length black leather boots, a short black skirt, and a pink blouse open at the top so that it showed her cleavage. She walked over to the bed and lifting her skirt to reveal she was not wearing any panties, took Paris's cock out and got on top of him.

'I am on fire for you,' she said, 'and the fire rages inside me more and more so that my pussy needs a constant pounding with your cock. I am going to ride you and grip you with these boots, I want to feel you gush hot come inside my cunt from your hard throbbing cock.'

In trying to devour Paris, Francesca became devoured by desire. He filled her with satiation and left her tingling with arousal. And all the time Flora became more jealous and suspicious. And Paris sensed behind Francesca's carnal pleasure lurked the shadow of something else.

#

Then one day Mr Agostino arrived. Paris saw his suitcases in the hallway of the apartment building and one glance at his chauffeur told him who he was.

Mr Agostino was standing in the marble hallway smoking a cigar and his chauffeur sat in the car. He was well muscled and behind him sat a large burly man. And Paris knew that Francesca was the wife of a dangerous man. He left the apartment, but not without Mr Agostino seeing him.

Later that day Paris met Francesca at a restaurant for lunch.

'My husband is back and I can't see you for a few days,' she said.

'I saw him earlier.'

'I am so frustrated.'

'We can find somewhere to meet.'

That evening while Mr Agostino met some business colleagues, Paris fucked Francesca at a hotel. They ate some fruit while taking a bath. Paris cut some juicy peaches with a knife, and placed the moist slices on Francesca's tongue. She sucked his cock, her arse in the air, and he massaged her clit. He fucked her for an hour on the bed, licking her pussy and then pumping it with his cock. After she came she looked at her watch and said, 'I must go, if he finds me gone he will become suspicious.'

She began to dress.

'What does your husband do?'

'Oh he exports things.'

'From Naples?'

'From everywhere.'

'Is he a dangerous man?'

Francesca looked at Paris and pulled on her shoes, then she blew a kiss at him. Paris was going into the bathroom as she opened the door. The chauffeur and the burly man Paris had seen earlier were standing in the corridor. They walked into the room and the chauffeur grabbed Francesca's arm.

'Mr Agostino wants to talk to you,' he said.

'Let me go.'

'You too,' the chauffeur said, pointing at Paris.

'I just need to use the toilet.'

Paris closed the door and emerged a minute later. He got his jacket from the chair in the bedroom and put it on.

The burly man took him by the arm. They escorted Paris and Francesca to a limousine and drove them to the apartment where Paris had fucked Francesca countless times. Mr Agostino sat waiting in the living room, cigar in his hand.

'So is this the man who has been making a fool of me?' he said.

Paris and Francesca were standing in front of him. The chauffer and bodyguard had left them alone with Mr Agostino.

'Making a fool of you?' Francesca said.

'What were you doing in the hotel with him?'

'Excuse me, Mr Agostino,' Paris said, 'I know how this must look, but I am visiting Rome and wanted to offer some business to your wife.'

'Business to my wife?'

'Yes, you see, I am a photographer and I want to take some pictures of Rome for her business. I am only here for a few days and she declined, saying you would object.'

'My wife has no business.' Mr Agostino stood up. 'Pictures? I have some pictures to show you.'

And he opened his attaché case, and placed one after the other on the table in front of him. Paris stared down at the shots of him walking with Francesca and of him fucking her at the apartment.

'These were taken yesterday,' Mr Agostino said.

He walked over to the door and opened it. Francesca was crying as the chauffeur and the burly man led Paris away. They took him down to the street and sat him in the limousine. Then they drove him out of Rome. Paris didn't ask where they were taking him, he watched the streets of the ancient city through the window.

At a deserted junction he reached into his jacket pocket and pulled the knife he had used to cut fruit. He could smell the peach juice on it as he stabbed the bodyguard in the carotid artery, then reached forward and sliced the driver's neck. He cut deeply, knowing he only had one chance. The windscreen was dripping with blood as he unlocked the doors and got out of the car.

He hailed a taxi in a nearby street and returned to his hotel, asking the driver to wait. Flora was at college and he left a note that read, 'Urgent business calls me away, I am sorry. I have settled the bill and strongly suggest you move out, since there are some people who want me dead.' Then he packed his few things and travelled to the airport, where he booked a flight to Madrid.

MANIAC AT THE AIRPORT.

This time Paris kept to himself on the flight. He avoided the glances of attractive women on the plane, and watched the sky outside his window as he left Italy behind, for he was travelling to Madrid, the woman with a savage heart as he thought of her, and he contemplated the sexual adventures he would have when he was there.

The plane touched down and Paris collected his luggage, stepping out into the throng of people holding up cards with names on them, none of them his. He felt like a sexual matador. He was alone again and free to seduce whom he wanted. He stopped for a glass of wine, a cold Rioja at the airport as he contemplated his next movements. And as he sat there a commotion broke out. Paris looked through the crowd to detect what was happening.

A young man with ragged hair was shouting at a crowd of tourists. Paris did not understand what he was saying, since music was playing in the restaurant and the man was some distance away, but soon the police became involved and Paris finished his drink, deciding to leave the airport and find a hotel.

As he walked past the crowd he saw a police officer strike the man on the head. He fell to the ground, clutching his temple and stared up at the officer in shock. Blood was pouring from his head. Paris stood there for a moment, feeling like a passer-by in life, a man at the edge of other's lives. He thought of all the women he'd seduced and left and he wondered if he would ever find any permanency. He decided to intervene.

Pushing his way through the crowd of people who watched this scene, some with their hands to their faces in shock, some laughing, Paris walked up the baton-wielding officer, and said, 'I know this man, what do you mean by hitting him?'

The officer was an officious large man with a heavy growth of stubble, who looked at Pars and said, 'Know him? He is a maniac. How do you know him? And who are you?'

'I am a diplomat here on business and he is the son of a friend of mine. Shall I relieve him from you?'

'Hm. Diplomat, where are your papers?

'I had them stolen, and that is why I approached you as an officer, to report the theft, then I saw what was happening. Surely there has been some misunderstanding here.'

'Well, he is always causing trouble, you better get him out of here and to his father.'

Paris reached out a hand and helped the young man to his feet. He was dirty and he smelt of sweat and wine. He stared at Paris in amazement.

'Come on we can get a taxi,' Paris said.

'You better report the theft to the local police station, here,' the officer said, showing Paris a map. 'We have to maintain order at the airport.'

As Paris walked through the crowds to the exit door wondering why he had helped a stranger in this way the young man said, 'I was telling them they were filthy animals, all the police are, and they began hitting me.'

Paris led him outside into the intense heat and looked for a taxi. As he stood there a Jeep drew up and a woman wearing tight faded denim shorts, a white blouse tied around her navel, and sunglasses jumped out.

'Frederico,' she said. 'What has happened to you?'

'The police hit me,' the young man said.

'You will need some stitches.'

'This man helped me.'

She turned to Paris then and lowered her sunglasses. And as she took in his fair features Paris saw her blink.

'I must thank you for helping my brother.'

'You are welcome, there was no need for them to hit him.'

'There is never any need for them to do that.'

'My name is Paris Tongue,' he said, holding out his hand.

'Esperanza Senza.'

Paris took her in. She was young, perhaps in her early thirties, and brown. Her tanned feet held a sensuality in their shape, as did her hands, and he glimpsed the outline of her nipples beneath her blouse. She stood there with her dark eyes locked on Paris's face and he smelt desire rising from her skin, the desire of a woman who knew no bounds in passion.

'Well, I will look for a taxi,' Paris said.

'Where are you staying?'

'I don't know yet, have you any recommendations?'

'Yes, stay with us, it is the least I can do to return your favour, we have a large house with plenty of space.'

'I would be imposing.'

'Not at all. It really is huge, too large for me and Frederico, but first we need him to get some stitches, come with us to the hospital.'

SEX CLUB.

AFTER THE HOSPITAL, WHERE PARIS WATCHED ESPERANZA'S dutifulness towards Frederico with interest since she seemed unmaternal in the extreme, they went to her huge house in the outskirts of Madrid, past Salamanca. Esperanza drove fast, passing through red lights, the wind in her hair, and they entered a gated garden at the end of which stood a huge villa. Esperanza pulled the Jeep to an abrupt stop, spraying gravel from the hot tyres.

'Welcome to the villa where you can do anything you want,' she said.

Paris got out and looked at the huge slice of land the house occupied.

'We are here situated near one of the wealthiest areas of our city, but outside it, for you have entered a world entirely on its own, with its own view of modern society,' Esperanza said.

Paris walked up the steps with her, his case in his hand and his jacket slung over the other arm.

It was a hot day and when they got inside Frederico said, 'I am going to bed and then to swim.'

Paris stood in the cool of marble hallway and watched as Esperanza kicked off her sandals and led him through to the kitchen.

'I imagine you are hungry or thirsty?'

'A cool glass of wine perhaps.'

'I have some chilled Albarino.'

'Perfect. I really must thank you for your hospitality.'

Esperanza pulled the cork from the bottle, her cleavage jutting out of her blouse, her nipples heavy against the cotton.

'I must thank you. My brother is different, shall we say, and the authorities do not like him, most people would not have helped him and I owe you a debt of gratitude.'

'You have nothing to be grateful for.'

'I am though, and I want to find a way to show you how much,' she said, handing him a glass of wine. 'Frederico is always going to the airport, he thinks the police there are animals and he provokes them.'

'Then I am glad I arrived when I did. A more enticing welcome than the one you are giving me could not be imagined.'

'To enticement, to pleasure,' she said, raising her glass.

'To a beautiful hostess, and all that she desires.'

They sipped their wine and held each other's gaze.

'Are you hungry or shall I show you to your room? I want to take a swim before my guests arrive for the evening's session.'

'Session?'

'Oh I shall tell you all about it Paris, I think you will fit right in.'

'A salad would be nice, but I would like to unpack.'

She placed her hand on his shoulder.

'Then bring your glass and I will take you to your room, follow me.'

He did, up the long marble staircase. He watched the movement of her tight buttocks and enjoyed the view he was afforded of the gap between her legs, a shape that made him long to remove her clothes and taste her pussy. Paris was becoming aroused as she led him along a corridor to a large room overlooking a swimming pool in a courtyard. It was lavishly appointed, with silk sheets and antique furniture and as Esperanza stood by the open window, he could make out the contour of her breasts. He imagined her naked, her firm body and wet cunt, and he pictured her with a full dark bush of hair.

'Come downstairs when you have unpacked and I will lay out a plate of tapas, the best Spanish tapas a man can eat, then you can join me for swim.'

'What is it you do here?'

'You will see, Paris, and do more than see.'

And so she left him and he unpacked and got in the shower, changing into a light pair of summer trousers and a short sleeved shirt.

As he combed his blonde hair he heard the noise of splashing from below, and gazed out at the flowers that climbed the walls around the swimming pool.

Someone was swimming and he saw them place a hand on the steps. A woman climbed out and walked over to a lounger. She was naked, with full breasts, shapely hips and a shaven cunt. She picked up a towel and began drying herself, the afternoon sun kissing her skin. She had full buttocks and dark nipples. She lay down on a lounger and spread her legs, inserting her finger inside herself and began to masturbate. Paris stood there sipping the last of his wine as she rubbed herself more and more vigorously, until she brought herself to climax. He could see the pink of her pussy in the golden sunshine, and drops of come glistening on her dark pubic hair. It made him want to go down and thrust his cock in.

He watched her get up and go inside. Then he went downstairs in search of Esperanza.

He found her in the kitchen laying out an assortment of Spanish chorizo, olives, ensaladilla rusa, and squid.

She poured him another glass of Albarino.

'Have you met our guest?' she said.

'I have met no one yet apart from you,' Paris said.

'No naked women below your window?'

'Yes I did see her.'

'Quite a lot of her I imagine?'

'She seems refreshingly unabashed, who is she?'

'Antonina.'

'You mentioned more guests are coming this evening.'

'Yes.'

'And you mentioned a session.'

'I run a sex club.'

'That explains Antonina's evident lack of inhibition.'

'Oh, was she masturbating?'

'She seemed to enjoy it.'

'She likes to be watched, she probably knew you were watching her. It stems from her husband's lack of interest in her. She came to me seeking advice. He never looks at her when she undresses. I encouraged her to expose herself and show her sexuality. She is attractive, no?'

'She is.'

'You sound hesitant, not your type?'

'I don't have a type.'

'No I suspect you don't, Paris.'

He sat and ate the tapas.

'This is good, fresh and a good balance of flavours.'

Esperanza sat on the back of a chair with her feet on the seat, her legs parted, and held his gaze as she drank her wine. He could see the shape of her inner thighs and the tight shorts against her pussy without lowering his eyes. Behind her he noticed the picture of a man on the wall. He seemed familiar to Paris. Esperanza noticed him looking at the picture.

'That is Georges Bataille, I am his illegitimate granddaughter,' she said.

'He wrote Erotism,' Paris said.

'My grandfather is perhaps responsible for who I am and what I do, since being brought up by parents who rebelled against his rebellion led me to a life that took a path enjoyed by few. I eat a rare fruit each day, like a man who licks the finest cunt at dawn, I am his inheritor, and I am carrying forward the discoveries he made in the world of flesh.'

'So what does the sex club do?'

'It allows men and women to liberate themselves from their sexual shackles. They come here, they fuck, they walk around naked and they return to their lives altered and greater than they were before. I help them find their orgasms, the ones they never knew they could achieve.'

'I believe Reich founded much of his psychoanalytic theory on the orgasm.'

'Paris you are true follower of fuck, for this is the villa fuck and there is no embarrassment saying it. It is the highest thing we are capable of, my body is mine to use and share with whom I want, you will be a part of our gathering tonight, but first, once your food is settled you will swim with me, but you must swim naked.'

Paris sipped his wine and looked at Esperanza, this liberated women who claimed she knew every inch of her sexual being, and he pictured her in the throes of orgasm, a dark priestess of sexuality, his, beneath him, his cock pounding the walls of her cunt, and he knew he could take her to heights she had never dreamed possible. And it also occurred to him in that moment that showing her things she did not know, things he had learned on the streets and while fucking the wealthy wives of bored husbands might alter her perception of herself and that could possibly injure her complacency. Paris considered that inasmuch as he enjoyed fucking women and giving them pleasure, he also enjoyed altering them, as if a piece of his unknown father had crept inside his gigolo's heart and lay there like a malicious gangster clutching a stiletto knife.

Esperanza looked at him as she fingered the top button on her blouse.

'My grandfather said, "Eroticism around us is so violent, it intoxicates hearts with so much force – to conclude, its abyss is so deep within us - that there is no celestial opening which does not take its form and its fever from it." I enjoy the body every day, I seek orgasms every minute.'

'I believe he also wrote, "I want to have my throat slashed while violating the girl to whom I will have been able to say: you are the night." It is the erotic night of which I speak.'

'You know his work. You also know what it means, what this building is for and my desire, you know the real sexual ecstasy.'

'Your desire.'

'To be transformed by orgasm.'

'It is a certain kind of orgasm that you seek.'

'It is.'

'Your need has not been fulfilled.'

'Perhaps you can do it for me.'

'You are talking of the religion of sex, of an ecstasy that elevates your identity.'

'You know what my grandfather wrote about and you know me, Paris.'

'I knew a woman who enjoyed him, among other things, I have a good memory.'

And Paris recalled Maria Revel, a distant echo of his life from long ago. He recalled her taking his erect penis in her hand and being his first fuck, an older seductress intent on squeezing the come from a young stud. He remembered her sitting on the bed and gently pulling the towel from him and taking him in her mouth, then inside her. She read Bataille all the time and used to quote that line to him, and Paris always thought it missed the secret ingredient, that of the ruthless nature of seductions, and he knew in his soul that it was the erotic talent of a pickpocket that allowed him to steal women's inhibitions from them as if he were unhooking their bras without them noticing. His sleight of hand was the trick of a mental conjurer, for Paris knew that pleasure began in the mind and desire needed licence to swell.

'His observation,' Esperanza said, 'means to me that he was aware of that real need in men to violate a woman's body, and I know that the way to tame a man is to hold his cock in your hand as you question him about his very deep rooted sense of anger towards woman, for she is always desired.'

'I am not sure all men carry that, some perhaps.'

'I once cured a serial rapist by sucking his cock while talking to him about his need to violate women, he became a high ranking priest and now will only masturbate if I watch him. So he comes to me and I sit in a chair while he gets his penis out and rubs it, I watch and then I wipe the come from it, I do not fuck him or engage in any form of intercourse, he is a fuller man than before, that is all thanks to my grandfather's teaching and his insights into the nature of eroticism.'

'I think there is more to sex than violation, Esperanza.'

'Yes there is but I still believe the cock of man must be tamed by the true and hidden cunt.'

'You mean the cunt of the mind?'

'Yes,' she said, standing up and stretching her arms. 'You seem far away, Paris.'

'I was recalling a woman whom I lost my virginity to, Maria Revel, she shared some of your beliefs. I lost contact with her but knew she also thought men needed taming. She was a harlot and quite beautiful. I heard years later she set a restaurant up in France and used to humiliate a dwarf who worked for her by sitting on his face while she prepared the dishes, chopping carrots while he licked her cunt. She had, as I recall, a particularly strong odour and lips that would suck a man's cock inside her and swallow it up if it wasn't up to the job. The dwarf violated her. But then her form of taming may be interpreted as humiliation and that was his revenge, the bed fellow of sexual passion. So her story was to be violated by dwarf with a huge penis. Apparently that is why she selected him for a cunt stool, because of his size.'

'But you see he had to stick his cock inside her against her permission.'

'No he used an aubergine she was preparing to make into a moussaka. Maria was raped by an aubergine, the dwarf beat his dick off into her hair, saying she needed to be bald, as bald as the head of a penis, and he shaved her head. Then he put her across his knee and spanked her. Apparently, she enjoyed the spanking, she had nicely toned buttocks and she played with herself as he thrashed her, coming as she ran her fingers inside her pussy. All of this was told to me by a most disreputable source and may of course be apocryphal.'

'But it still supports my belief that young men need to be shown the correct uses of their cocks, then they may satisfy women.'

'Are you of the school that believes the cunt is the source of sexual pleasure?'

'Yes and no, but you are not far off. And what school are you of, Paris?'

'Seduction. I am of course self-taught but I learned at the hands of the lustful mistress life herself.'

'And you, Paris, are you of the night?'

'No, I am of the day of passion on tangled sheets, that moment when you lose yourself utterly to the orgasm.'

'Then you will join us tonight, I have men and women coming to learn their pleasures.'

'And what of Frederico?'

'You mean where does my brother fit into this? He doesn't. I look after him. He sometimes watches the naked women and hides in the bushes playing with his prick.'

'Is he your only family?'

'He is. And what of your family, Paris?'

'I am the bastard child of a killer, I have none that I know of.'

'Come on, let us swim.'

She rose from her chair and Paris followed her through the cool marble hall and along a corridor to a door that opened onto the courtyard. It was a violently hot afternoon, and crickets beat a melody in the fields that lay at the outskirts of the villa. The sun was beating down on them from an intense blue sky as Esperanza stripped.

She untied her blouse and removed it. She had large brown breasts with dark nipples and she watched as Paris took off his shirt and pulled down his trousers. She dropped her eyes to his crotch as she unzipped her denim shorts and stepped out of them naked. She had a full black bush of hair. She walked over to Paris as he slipped out of his jockeys and looked at his cock.

Then she took it in her hand and rubbed it.

'That is a real penis Paris, I knew you were a stranger with a gift, it is the kind of cock that may well fit my cunt for a good hard fucking.'

Paris slid his finger inside her.

'You are wet Esperanza, it seems your pussy is ready for some action.'

'First we swim, tonight you come to my bedroom.'

She led him into the pool by his cock, holding it until they stood to their chests in the blue water.

'I will enjoy you, I will rub you and suck you, fuck you and pound your cock until all you know is my cunt, for she is a special cunt.'

'I will find a way to make her sing as she comes, to give you the finest orgasms, to take you to that deep electric ecstasy.'

RICHARD GODWIN

She rubbed his cock, looking at it through the water as she touched herself. Then she began to swim. Paris watched her part her legs and kick with them, her pussy visible below her toned arse and her black pubic hair. Then he swam too, enjoying the cool water and the afternoon sun. Afterwards as they dried themselves, Paris saw Antonina naked on a balcony with her finger inside herself as she watched them.

THE SEDUCTION OF ESPERANZA.

T HAT EVENING AS CRICKETS POUNDED OUT THEIR EROTIC melody and night fell, awash with stars, Paris stepped outside and wandered the gardens of the ancient villa's estate. It seemed to him imbued with the sensual pleasures of Esperanza, as if her desire lay embedded in the stones and gardens that adorned her establishment. The air was heavy with the smell of magnolias and thyme, and the place seemed set apart from the modern world, an orgy of ancient desire and fecundity, a transgression without sin, a precise point on the map of human pleasure.

And Paris felt aroused. He briefly thought of Flora and her body and his attention turned immediately to his new found conquest, the whore with high ideas, whom he would turn into his concubine for as long as he desired. And it occurred to him that he was a man for whom attachments held no appeal, a sexual outsider who profited from the prisons that others inhabited as they lusted for Eros and all he brought to the world of pleasures, of unfettered sex on lustful sheets.

Lights came on at the back of the villa as Paris stood there, and he could see men and women gathering outside. And so he walked back and was introduced to the guests. Formally dressed men and women stood with glasses of Cava, talking of the night, as Esperanza walked among them, touching them, kissing them. Then the session began.

'We have a new guest tonight,' she said. She walked over and touched Paris on the chest. 'Paris Tongue has joined us tonight.'

'Welcome Paris,' they murmured.

They seemed absurd actors in a sexual drama whose meaning they did not understand. Paris watched them as if they were tourists waiting for some main event, and he knew that the event they all sought was the orgasm, the destination of pleasure in the mind of man and woman.

And he knew that he was there for one reason, not to watch these men and women engage in sexual acts, but to seduce the hostess.

They stripped and began to touch one another, a heaving mass of flesh, some attractive, most not, licking and fucking there in the outdoors of the villa fuck. Paris watched for a while and then went inside knowing it may appear as modesty but the truth was it appeared ridiculous to him and too easy, a free dish when he wanted to trick his way into the best restaurant.

He toured the villa, with its bedrooms that seemed made for different sexual encounters, and he looked down at the garden full of naked men and women copulating while Esperanza watched. Then he went outside again and sat drinking Cava. Esperanza walked over to him.

'Are you shocked, Paris?'

'Not shocked, perhaps bored.'

'The appeal of all these bodies is lost on you?'

'Perhaps there is one body I want more than those.'

'These men and women are finding their liberation, I am, if you will, creating a revolution in the hearts and minds of the idle residents of Madrid. This is a city with Catholic guilt and inhibitions stifling the true passion of its nature. I let them fuck, enjoy one another and then return them to their lives.'

'Where their guilt and inhibitions wait for them.'

'Not they are changed here. Can you not see that?'

'I see their enjoyment. But real change happens not when someone else shows you the way to liberation, for you are no more than an authority figure, allowing them to indulge in things they would not otherwise. Without you here they would not have the chance to do these things, they would not have the seal of a beautiful sexual woman they all want to fuck.'

'There is no authority here.'

'There is, you just don't see it.'

'I am challenging all theory with the sex club.'

'Transgression reinforces the limit.'

'What are your limits, Paris?'

'I will show you later tonight.'

#

When all the men and women had left, had clothed their bodies and driven off in cars, Paris was left alone with Esperanza beneath the throbbing liquid night. They said little then, knowing one another's desire and not wishing to accentuate the extent of it, as if admission might bring loss of status and heartache. But Paris knew heartache was as alien to him as inhibition and he talked to her beneath the star strewn sky while the odour of her perfume rose from her flesh as if it was becoming warmer with his words.

She was wearing a low cut black dress, and her shoulders looked brown and muscular, and her breasts heaved beneath the material that seemed too tight to hold them in. Paris pictured her legs beneath it, and her cunt, and wondered if she was already wet and wearing any panties. This was now the erotic night, where he dwelled as the ghost lover. He was about to commit a revolutionary sexual act that would show his place in history.

Then he touched her. It was a simple gesture. He ran his hand along her arm and stopped at the side of her breasts. He rose and took her face in his hands and kissed her deeply on the mouth. He could tell from her hungry tongue she was aroused and he kissed her long enough to set her on fire. For he held back, his held his passion and desire deep inside him as if locked in a clenched fist and she felt it. What Paris was proving there was his place in erotic history, that body of sensations and pleasure, it was there in Madrid, it was the deep Noir City. It was there in London and Paris, in Rome and all the other places he might venture. He was creating it with his hands, building it brick by brick, but there were building blocks of ecstasy. It was the eternal place of desire. It was deep because it existed in penetration. Paris penetrated their bodies and their minds, their hearts and their secret fantasies, he occupied them like an Emperor and they worshipped him because they had to. It was electric in intensity and as blue as the day in deep summer. Eros reigned, Paris gave. Esperanza yielded. She had to, she needed his hands on her skin.

Then they went inside and Esperanza fetched a bottle of chilled Rioja from the kitchen and they scaled the stairs to the bedroom full of lace and silk. It was like an exotic bordello. She poured them a glass each and they drank. Then Paris removed her dress and admired her body. He touched her nipples lightly, delicately, then took them in his mouth. Esperanza unzipped his trousers and took his cock in her hand.

He lowered her G-string and inserted his finger inside her. She bent and sucked him, taking his cock deep into her mouth. Paris was rubbing Esperanza's clit when she began to gasp. They were short bursts of sound full of depravity and they told him exactly how she wanted to be fucked. He led her to the bed and she lay down, parted her legs and she took his head and conducted it to her full bush and wet lips. As Paris began to lick her pussy Esperanza thrust her cunt into his mouth and cried, 'Eat me, eat my cunt and then fuck me hard with your huge cock.'

He licked and rubbed her until she shot a bucket of come all over the bed and she lay covered in sweat, panting. Her lips were sparkling and her nipples stood erect like bullets on her brown breasts, as Paris rolled her over and raised her tight arse so she was thrusting her lips at him between her parted legs, and he began to rub her clit again while he inserted his thumb inside her arsehole. Esperanza screamed in ecstasy. Her moans became deeper, more depraved, and Paris realised he was penetrating to the core of the woman.

Esperanza turned around and grabbed Paris's cock.

'Fuck me!' she said.

She lay back and spread her legs and Paris entered her cunt slowly, inserting his cock inch by inch until her groans became deranged. He could hear she was reaching a height of ecstasy unknown to her and he began to fuck her, licking and kissing her nipples as he did. He increased his rhythm, plunging his cock deeper and deeper into her wet cunt. And as Esperanza came again her cunt squeezed his cock hard and Paris lifted her off the bed as she clung to him and he filled her cunt with come, pumping it inside her.

They rose and drank more wine and Paris licked it from her nipples as she groaned with desire. Esperanza took his cock in her hand again and rubbed it until it was erect and Paris sat down and she got on top of him and lowered her cunt onto his cock and rode him, her face full of a desire that was deranged, her body throbbing.

'In pleasure there is pain,' she said, over and over again as she filled herself with ecstasy, 'I fuck until I ache.'

She got on her knees and parted her thighs and she crawled across the floor with a desire so furious she felt the tug in insanity at the corner of her mind. Then she stood up and gazed at her love god there before her with the eyes of idolatry and disdain for the things of ordinary mortals, they were altering time that night of ecstasy, she took him in her hand and got on the bed again.

She rode him and Paris fucked her into the night until it was almost dawn. It was as if Esperanza wanted to test how many times he could get erect, but there were no limits for Paris. Eventually Esperanza slept from exhaustion and Paris lay in the bed next to her smelling the odour of her pleasure, a smell like the soil of rich earth deep in woods after a heavy fall of rain when the ground has been parched too long. She smelt of the burst seeds of flowers heavy in the air on a summer evening. Fecund place of pleasure satiated by his hands. Hot hard place of passion and sexual desire.

He awoke before her and looked at her face. And he knew he had unlocked the secret Esperanza. He rose and made some coffee and she followed soon afterwards, wearing his shirt over her naked body and entering the kitchen with the blur of her cunt clear against the white material.

They drank coffee and then Paris went to shower. As he was getting dressed Esperanza came into the bedroom looking flustered.

'What is the matter?' Paris said.

'Frederico's missing, I have looked everywhere for him.'

FLORA IS FOLLOWED FROM THE AIRPORT.

WHEN PARIS LEFT THE GIULIO CESARE HOTEL IN ROME FLORA was standing outside. She had left her classes early, suspicious of his lack of punctuality and sure he was having an affair. When she saw him get into a taxi with his case she followed in another taxi. And she watched him enter the crowd at the airport and saw him book a flight to Madrid.

She almost approached him to slap his face but she withdrew and travelled back, sobbing and angry. She drank all day and decided she would put him out of her mind, and went out to find the first man she liked and to fuck him. This resulted in an embarrassing encounter with a waiter who left her frustrated and unsatisfied, and craving Paris. She wanted to punish and fuck Paris and imagined riding his cock with a whip in her hand.

Then, back at the hotel, she saw his note and began to panic. She reprimanded herself, beating her thighs with a hairbrush until they bled, and screaming, 'Stupid cow!' at herself in the mirror.

The next morning she thought it through.

'Of course, Paris loves me, he wants to protect me, that is why he has gone away, and I must find him and reassure him of my love then we can be together.'

And so she packed.

#

Meanwhile when Mr Agostino's chauffeur and bodyguard did not return from their job of killing Paris their boss became suspicious. He had entertained himself with the ritual humiliation of his trophy wife by making her suck his cock while he sang opera in a strange growl.

Francesca was faced with his fat groin as he belted out La donna e mobile. She tried to suck it, but eventually stood up and said, 'I am sick of you singing while I stare at your shrivelled cocktail sausage for a cock, I want a big hard prick inside me.'

Luigi slapped her hard, knocking her over. She fell onto a coffee table. When she got up she flew at him and he punched her, knocking out two of her teeth.

'If you are not careful, you slut I will make you ugly then no one will fuck you, remember your place.'

He sent out two of his men, Carlo and Marco, to find his missing car. They were two of his nastiest hired killers, men who enjoyed inflicting pain and suffering and who had a penchant for spilling blood. They tracked the limousine using the location of the chauffeur's mobile, and found him and the bodyguard dead at the deserted junction.

'There is no one around,' Carlo said, peering in the window.

'Someone will find them soon and call the police.'

They sped back to their boss who ranted, 'Find that fucking prick, cut his cock off!'

He told them where Paris had been staying, since one of his men had been following Paris and Francesca for a day before Luigi confronted them, and Carlo and Marco travelled to there while he arranged for his limousine to be collected. They bribed the receptionist for information about their guests and discovered that Paris had been sharing a room with Flora.

And they saw her leaving with a suitcase.

They followed her to the airport and got on the same flight as her to Madrid, staying in communication with their boss who said, 'Bring him back and I will kill him in front of my wife!'

As Flora stepped out of customs at Madrid airport there was a commotion surrounding Frederico, who had returned to the airport believing that Paris was a blonde god sent to save him from the police animals.

He was yelling, 'His beauty exceeds all limits, all women yearn for him, Paris saved me!'

When Flora heard Paris's name mentioned she stopped and took note of this strange young man. Frederico was about to get arrested as she walked up to him and said, 'Do you know Paris?'

'Yes, he is with my sister now.'

Flora got out her mobile phone and showed him a picture she had taken of Paris.

'Is this him, is this the man you say is with your sister?'

'Yes, he is the one.'

'Can you take me to him?'

'Of course he is at the villa fuck.'

A police officer was approaching Frederico as he said this.

'If you don't leave now we will arrest you,' he said.

'Come with me,' Flora said, taking Frederico's arm and walking outside with him.

Frederico had driven there in one of his sister's cars and now took Flora to Paris, as Carlo and Marco tailed them in a taxi.

Flora wondered what Frederico had meant by the villa fuck and her jealousy at the idea of Paris with another woman began to claw at her desire for him.

Paris was drinking a glass of chilled Rioja that hot day when the men and women arrived for the early session. Esperanza had realised she had no time to go to the airport in search of her brother and she got ready for her session of the Avenue of Women amid the lush gardens and heat.

Paris stood on the balcony of his room looking down at the land as Esperanza greeted her guests. Then he watched the women strip and stand in lines that ran along the gardens, a body of naked flesh amid the fecund Spanish soil. A hundred naked bodies stretched all the way down to the tilled fields that lay parched in the relentless Spanish sun.

And Paris thought how dull most peoples' lives were, a simple matter of work and copulation. And he thought how he catered to the hidden fantasies of women and how having seduced the mistress of this sexual drama he would move on to something new, and something different. And for a moment he wondered if that would be love. He sipped his wine, thinking that it was usually lust dressed in its best clothes, while beneath the hem of the skirt lay a wet and hungry snatch.

He went down to the gardens and looked at them all, naked, alone, desiring something more from their lives than the small things they held at home and enjoyed in the dark. Esperanza was talking to them, these women who stood there naked, touching their bodies as Paris heard a car draw up.

'Now touch yourselves among the gardens of the villa fuck,' Esperanza said, 'finger those pussies until you water the soil with come.'

Flora entered the grounds of the villa following Frederico, to see this strange sight of a hundred masturbating women, while Carlo and Marco got out of the taxi chuckling.

'Wait here,' Carlo said to the taxi driver, 'and we will pay you double.'

The driver nodded and lit a cigarette.

'This won't take long,' Marco said to Carlo as they walked in.

Paris saw Flora and immediately knew he was in trouble, not from her, but he sensed she had brought

Agostino's men with her and he went upstairs to gather his few things and leave.

As he did so he saw Carlo and Marco enter the grounds of the villa from his window and he knew then that he was being hunted. He watched them stand and stare at the naked women and he scanned the landscape thinking of how he would get away. He saw the taxi waiting outside and he saw Carlo and Marco walk towards the villa.

And Paris felt angry that Agostino assumed he could kill him and that he had been followed. He went downstairs to the kitchen by a back staircase and he got the largest knife from a drawer. He set his case down in the hall and walked outside while Carlo and Marco looked for him in the empty villa.

'What is this place with all these naked women?' Carlo said.

'I don't know but we can fuck a few after we kill him.'

'How do you plan to do it, since we have no guns?'

'Choke him to death.'

Outside Frederico was explaining to Flora what Esperanza did there and she saw them and walked over to her brother.

'Where have you been?'

'I met this woman, she is looking for Paris.'

The two women eyed one another jealously.

Just then Paris emerged in a white shirt and trousers. He walked over to Flora, kissed her on the mouth and said, 'I'm sorry but you have brought trouble with you.'

Then he kissed Esperanza and said, 'Thank you for putting me up.'

'In my villa or in my cunt?' she said.

'Paris, what is this about?' Flora said.

Carlo and Marco emerged from the villa and Paris ran, ducking behind a wall. They raced after him, but Frederico put out his foot and tripped Marco, who fell heavily on the ground. He got up, wiping blood from his face and punched Frederico. Esperanza screamed and clawed skin from his face.

As Carlo got to the corner of the wall Paris emerged and sank the knife into his heart. Carlo stared in amazement at him and staggered about, spraying blood everywhere as Paris ran into the Avenue of Women. And Marco followed him.

There amid the naked flesh of the women Paris lost his pursuer. Marco couldn't see him as the women all jostled him and he pushed his way past their naked breasts. They reached for his cock in their sexual frenzy and Marco pushed them aside, smelling the heavy odour of cunt in the hot air.

Paris was faster than Marco and ran through the Avenue of Women and back to the villa where he grabbed his case and ran to the taxi.

'Paris!' Flora shouted after him. 'Wait I am coming with you.'

'Where are you going?' Esperanza yelled. 'Who are these men chasing you?'

'Take me to the airport,' Paris said to the driver, who was nodding off.

'I am already booked by the two men who went in there,' the driver said, pointing to the villa.

'They've decided to stay, they're taking a holiday.'

'They said they'd pay me double.'

'So will I and I'll give you a tip if you get me there fast.'

'You'll be there in no time.'

The driver started the engine. As he drove away Paris glanced behind him and saw Marco running out of the villa soaked in sweat.

But the avenue that led to the villa faded from sight and the Avenue of Women faded from memory as Paris sat in the taxi. And he bore the knowledge of his own deficit with him all the way though the crowds, which were empty now with the absence of Frederico, the maniac who had taken him to the villa fuck and who had brought danger with him.

Paris walked up to the first airline he saw, Lufthansa, and he booked a ticket to the first town he saw, because it was all the same to him. He ignored the attention of the woman who checked him in and sat thinking all the way there. And what he thought about was how he might change his life now. And he wondered what he would find in Düsseldorf.

KINKY.

Each time he left a city it faded from his mind, as did the women he left behind. For Paris lived in his own city, it was his sexual Empire mined from the groans of their ecstasy.

Düsseldorf was a marked contrast to the places Paris had been to before. Neat and orderly, lying at the centre of the Lower Rhine basin, at first it reminded Paris of a woman who had never ventured beyond kissing into the wilder sexual acts he knew so well. It was clean, and to Paris its sexuality seemed to belong to the hygienic fuck. Yet as Paris took the city in, another flavour emerged. He sensed among the men and women a desire for acts at odds with their natures. Where the river Düssel flows into the Rhine at Düsseldorf, Paris felt a depravity beneath the tidy looks he met from the women in the street, as if a licentious urge was copulating there with the facade of sexual morality. There were brutal fantasies here. The women wanted to be dominated, they needed cock in the long hot afternoons.

As he observed Düsseldorf, and penetrated its sleeping heart, Paris sensed the hidden element he often detected in women. The city seemed the stage of a well secluded brothel, as if behind its facade lay the theatre of orgy. And he sensed that the women he observed longed for something unusual. Paris could taste the sexual double life that characterised the city's night.

He analysed the population, as if it contained a hidden message. The German women were well built, some large, many attractive, but they seemed too clean to him and he searched for the whore among them. He sat in cafes drinking coffee while large men swigged beer and he observed the way the women of the city spoke. And he felt they wanted to be touched in a forbidden way, but one that left them safe with their pretence of morality. That ethical stance seemed to Paris a set of clothes beneath which lay the most enticing cunt, and he yearned to undress the demure woman of Düsseldorf to find the whore beneath and arouse her to her lascivious heart.

He knew that many of the women he saw would allow him to take them to a hotel and fuck them then return to their husbands. He could hear them groaning and screaming as they entered their sexual ecstasies. He could tell what their sexual appetites were and how they hid from them by day. And it seemed to him that each city he visited was the Noir City where sex lived by night. And Paris saw himself riding it as he rode the women he encountered as he seduced Europe.

One afternoon in a café he sat opposite an attractive large bosomed blonde woman who from time to time glanced at him as she spoke to her friend. Paris imagined undressing her and fucking her on a train as she gazed out of the window, her breasts bare to the air, her large arse slapping against his groin as he pounded her cunt.

He was running out of money and knew he would have to trade on his looks again, and that meant finding a woman with money. But Paris wanted to taste a different kind of sexual hunger from the next woman he fucked, he wanted something other than passion or need, which he had experienced countless times.

He wanted to fuck a woman who engaged in acts that stood at the edge of social propriety. And he was about to meet one.

#

He was walking through the Konigsallee and its fashion shops looking for wives with money, when he saw a woman leaning against the doorway of a shop looking at him. The shop was called 'Non-Vanilla' and Paris recognised at once the woman's interest in him. She was full busted, blonde, had intense green eyes that glimmered even at the distance that separated them, and she wore a sheer blouse open to her lace bra. Her generous cleavage jutted out above the cups, inviting the eye to wander downwards in search of her full nipples. Her tight black skirt outlined ample hips and she wore shiny black boots. Thinking about how he had not yet secured lodging for the night, Paris walked over to her.

He stood looking at the clothes in her window, then he turned to her. She seemed to be tempting him in sexually, as if he were a client and she were deciding on the price of her snatch that day, but Paris knew that what she was offering and what she wanted was not that simple, and the relationship he would have with her would carry with it the complications of a nature that lay outside the regular exchange of desire and touch.

'You're interested in my shop,' she said.

'I am looking for a place to stay.'

'What kind of area do you want? Düsseldorf is a mixed city, there are quiet areas, or perhaps you want to be among the noise and night life, of which there are any kinds.'

'I don't mind night life.'

'Come inside,' she said. 'I can look up a few hotels for you.'

He followed her into the shop, which was packed with expensive designer clothes for women.

'There are many hotels here, it depends how much you want to spend for a night. I am a landlady and in need of assistance in the shop,' she said. 'Where are you from?'

'Everywhere.'

'Everywhere? And do you have a name?'

'Paris Tongue.'

She held out a hand.

'Brigitte Kunze.'

'It is a pleasure to meet you Brigitte.'

'What are you doing in Düsseldorf?'

'Exploring the city.'

'Some people say the city is like the body of a woman, and you have to know how to reach the hidden parts, the parts where the real pleasure lies.'

Paris looked at Brigitte. Her eyes held the history of unusual needs, and he began to calculate with his gigolo's thinking how to satisfy them that she may be his hostess while he sojourned there, away from the past, anchorless, free to explore flesh while he remained young and desired.

'Is your house nearby?' he said.

'Yes, not far, I share it with my sister, and you can have your own room if you help me in the shop. It is an easy job, tending to the silly tastes of fashion-seeking women, although, I can't really have you helping them in the changing rooms. Let me see, well you can always shut your eyes.'

She laughed.

'The name of your shop indicates a taste in something beyond the ordinary.'

'Oh yes, there is the other part to it, behind the clothes you see in here.'

Brigitte walked to a door at the back of the shop and opened it. Paris followed her through to a room full of leather gear and whips.

LIPS.

THE HOUSE WAS SITUATED A FEW MINUTES' WALK FROM THE shop and Paris and Brigitte walked there in the bright sunshine.

'You seemed unsurprised by the other side of my shop,' she said. 'Many men are shocked, threatened by it.'

'Why would I be threatened?'

'Men like to think all a woman needs is the simple kind of pleasure they offer, the idea they their wife needs something else, something that seems split from their life is frightening. It is almost as if by engaging in acts deemed immoral or different the woman will become someone who will devour the man.'

'Exploring never scared me. I am sure you have already broken loose from your moorings and engage in acts that lie outside the ordinary.'

Brigitte stopped and looked at Paris.

'I can always tell,' she said, 'when a man is able to read what I do and who I am. How could you tell with me?'

'It's in your eyes.'

'I am well known in certain parts of Düsseldorf. In fact, among my clientele, who number the wives of wealthy men, the things I say get circulated like a rare coin.'

'Do you simply cater to the women here who like bondage or who seek something different to the missionary position?'

'I do more than cater, as you will find out. Welcome to the real Düsseldorf, Düsseldorf the slut.'

The house was set behind some old iron gates that were rusting and had acquired a greenish tinge. Brigitte led Paris through the garden and up the stairs to the front door. It was a large house. Inside, it was full of artefacts from German history, and Paris admired the paintings and furniture.

'I will show you your room,' Brigitte said, and led him upstairs to a room overlooking the gardens.

Painting of erotic scenes covered the walls, men fucking women, maids with their skirts hitched up and large buttocks exposed, men whipping their backsides, pounding their cunts with huge penises and large women sitting on smaller men's faces with massive wet cunts.

Paris set his case down. He looked at Brigitte, and he thought of how many cities he had toured simply by picking women up and engaging with their lifestyles, and he knew this one's would be different. She was standing there with her hands on her hips, her large breasts pushing against her blouse.

'Do you want to wash?' she said.

'I haven't eaten for a while, perhaps I can have some food first.'

'I'll make you something. Plenty of time for washing, Paris.'

She took him to the kitchen which was spotless, and made him a sandwich with Bockwurst and salad.

'Have some wine, from the Rhine,' she said, fetching a bottle from the fridge and two glasses. 'This is a Franz Künstler Riesling Spätlese Hochheimer Kirchenstück, a fine wine.'

Paris sipped it, enjoying its pineapple flavour.

Brigitte sat opposite him, away from the table. She placed her feet on another chair and Paris caught a glimpse of her thighs.

As he ate the sandwich a woman entered the room. She was tall and dark haired, with dark eyes and she had a toned body clearly visible beneath the sleeveless midnight blue tunic blouse that stopped at the top of her thighs.

'Paris, meet my sister Heidi,' Brigitte said.

Heidi held out her hand to Paris who stood and shook it.

'He is staying with us,' Brigitte said.

'I should be more modestly dressed in the presence of guests,' Heidi said, sitting down. 'But then there's not much modesty in this house.'

'Not much modesty at all,' Brigitte said.

Brigitte's skirt was riding up her thighs and Paris caught a glimpse of her shaved pussy. And he realised he was in the middle of a sexual game, the play time of sisters.

He looked at her face and Brigitte held his gaze, as if she wanted his acknowledgment of what he had seen, and was trying to read his level of arousal.

'Paris will be helping in the shop,' she said to Heidi.

'And do you like women with unusual tastes?' Heidi said, standing up.

'How unusual?' Paris said.

Heidi glanced at her sister.

'It must be obvious to you that we are women who enjoy something different. There is nothing wrong with exploring our licentious natures, and with a man as handsome as, well, we must surely heighten our pleasures, so perhaps this afternoon we can show you the kind of things you may encounter while staying here.'

'I look forward to seeing you both at play.'

Paris went to his room to shower and change. He came down wearing a pair of blue trousers and a steel coloured shirt that accentuated his physique.

Brigitte was sitting in a low chair in the living room, reading a pornographic magazine. When Paris came in she glanced up, closed it and raising her leg, said, 'I think I have cut my toe.'

Her skirt clung to her ample thighs and Paris looked down at her foot.

'I see nothing there,' he said.

'What else do you see?'

Brigitte's pussy was exposed, and Paris looked at her full lips, and clit which protruded on her shaven cunt.

'I see a fine pair of lips on an aroused cunt, do you want me to tend to it?'

'And what would you do with a cunt like mine?'

Just then Heidi entered the room and sat on a chair adjacent to them. Paris stood looking down at Brigitte's pussy. She placed one finger inside her snatch, the other in her mouth. Then Paris touched her, running his hand down her thigh. He fingered her as Heidi raised her blouse to show him a shapely peach like cunt.

'Look at my clit, Paris,' Heidi said, 'do you know what I can do with my cunt? It is a muscle I can close hard on any prick I choose to let inside it, but I am fussy, preferring to play with myself. Look at the two sisters, does it make your prick stiff, watching us? I imagine your cock big and hard.'

Paris continued to rub Brigitte who was groaning louder as Heidi played with her cunt until it was dripping wet. Then Paris removed Brigitte's blouse. He touched her full breasts. He kissed and sucked her nipples and he continued rubbing her cunt.

Brigitte looked across at her sister and Paris noticed an expression of superiority on her face, as if Heidi was deprived of his attentions and Brigitte was the mistress of the situation. So Paris walked over to Heidi and said, 'May I touch this cunt?'

Heidi looked at him with wild animal eyes, and Paris detected in her a nature so extreme he imagined giving her deadly orgasms, for he knew she hadn't reached her sexual core and briefly it occurred to him that if he took her there she may become deranged, as if her sexuality was not socialised.

'Look at my cunt, isn't it the perfect shape?' she said, rubbing it. 'Do you think to stick your finger in there after it has been thrumming my sister's pussy?'

'Heidi, no, I want to insert my tongue in your beautiful cunt.'

Heidi took her hand away and Paris leant and began to lick her. It wasn't long before it was evident that she was becoming ferociously aroused, and she lunged her hips towards him, as if she wanted to cram her pussy inside his mouth.

'Oh your tongue is setting me on fire, yes, run it around my throbbing clit, can you taste me? I am so tasty I sometimes stick my finger inside myself and then suck it.'

Paris sucked and licked her pussy, thrusting his nimble tongue deep inside Heidi's quivering snatch. She lifted her blouse over her head, revealing ample breasts that Paris fondled, as she thrust her pussy into his mouth and screamed, 'Oh fuck, I am going to come, open your mouth Paris and drink my cunt juice.'

She sprayed a river of come out of her lips and Paris swallowed it. He stood up and said, 'I have drunk the fine wine of one sister's hungry cunt and now for the other's.'

Brigitte got up from the chair and glanced down at Heidi.

'I will sit on your face, Paris, then I will work your cock until it fills us both with come, can you pump your come into two women's cunts?'

'I will fill them with their distinct and separate pleasures.'

Paris got beneath Brigitte, placing his head on the chair she had sat on, as she lowered her dripping cunt onto his mouth and began to grind her clit across his lips. He inserted his tongue and heard her gasp, he licked and flicked her clit until she was screaming, as she played with her own breasts and then she let loose a torrent of come.

Paris stood up and looked at Brigitte panting as Heidi rose from her chair.

'Time for your hard cock, Paris,' she said, wagging a finger at him. 'Can you fulfil us further?'

'I look forward to fucking you both,' Paris said.

Heidi began to unzip his fly as Brigitte took Heidi's hand in hers.

'I'm having him first.'

'No, I want his cock inside me. I came before you.'

'No, that is not the way.'

'OK, we guess, how big he is and what it looks like and the winner gets to taste his cock, while the loser watches.'

'I say he is big and uncircumcised,' Brigitte said.

'Big and circumcised, now who is right?'

'Then let us see, Brigitte said, darting her hand down to Paris's crotch. His trousers already showed his size by the significant bulge. Heidi raced down to touch it too, and both women grappled with his pants to pull out his erect cock. Brigitte rubbed it while Heidi touched the tip.

'Big and circumcised,' Heidi said, 'I was right.

'He is big, he is huge enough to fill my ravenous cunt hole,' Brigitte said, 'and I want it straight in my snatch once he has fucked your pussy.'

'We used to argue over dolls now it is cock, 'Heidi said.

'Plaything penis give us orgasms,' Brigitte said.

And he looked into their yes and saw derangement there, the unhinged minds of women gorged to excess on physical pleasure. They were real whores. He knew the way to handle them. He'd known every kind of women. All different, all with certain territory they shared. He knew their hypocrisy before he fucked them.

They undressed him, unbuttoning his shirt and running their hands across his chest, then removing his trousers. Heidi played with his balls while Brigitte continued to rub his cock, until Heidi said, 'Enough, he is mine and my cunt is dripping wet. Fill me with your hard prick Paris, ride my pussy.'

Heidi lay back on the sofa and Paris entered her. He pumped her cunt with his throbbing cock, slowly, then harder, and faster, plunging deeper and deeper inside her until she screamed. Paris pulled out his cock and Brigitte glanced down to see it was still erect as Heidi lay there with her cunt gaping and her nipples standing out like bullets from her tits.

'That was the best orgasm I have ever had,' she said.

Brigitte took his cock in her hand.

'And look, he hasn't come, I am going to have the satisfaction of the first taste of his come and my cunt will lick it from the tip of his spurting knob.'

Heidi stood up, 'That is for me not you, I won, he needs to fuck me again and I will empty his balls.'

'Ladies,' Paris said, 'no need to argue, my cock is able to satisfy you both and to share equally between your fine and hungry cunts an ocean of come.'

'Really?' Heidi said.

Brigitte lay back on the sofa and Paris plunged his cock inside her, riding her snatch as he sucked her nipples.

'Oh my cunt is on fire,' she said, 'your cock slides inside me like a huge dido, your huge throbbing prick can go on for hours.'

Paris pumped her cunt until she came.

'Now me, come inside my pussy,' Heidi said, leaning and sucking Paris.

She took him deep into her mouth as she fingered herself.

Then Brigitte ran her tongue along the shaft of his cock and sucked him.

They lay back on the sofa.

Paris began to fuck Heidi again as Brigitte played with herself.

He fondled Brigitte's breasts as he pounded Heidi's cunt until he began to orgasm and he pumped come into Heidi's tight snatch. Then he pulled out and plunged his cock into Brigitte's pussy and shot the rest of his come inside her.

Both sisters lay there staring at him in amazement.

'I'd like to fuck you both from behind,' Paris said. 'Plunging my cock into your cunts while I enjoy the sight of your fine arses will be a great pleasure.'

TWO SISTERS.

Later that day they dined at a small restaurant called 'Musch'. Paris watched the two sisters as they eyed each other awkwardly, jealousy flickering at the edge of the conversation that was polite but barely able to contain the fact that they were resentful of one another. From time to time they reached across to pick food from his plate. And each time that they did one sister would glance at the other then back again at Paris.

Heidi wore a tight black skirt and blouse that complimented the shape of her full breasts. Brigitte wore a flowing dress beneath which Paris knew she wore no panties. Once she placed her foot up on his chair and he looked down at her full wet cunt as she licked a gherkin and chewed on it.

'Later I will take your cock in my mouth, then you can fuck my pussy again,' she said.

'My sister and I are nymphomaniacs,' Heidi said. 'We have always fucked men in huge numbers.'

'Yes we are high on sex, and Paris you will tend to both our pussies and tell us which one tastes the finest to your huge pounding cock. I want you to ride my cunt until you have emptied every drop of come inside me. I want to feel it shoot from your prick and fill me with its hot rush. I also want you to lick me for hours.'

'My pussy is tighter,' Heidi said, 'it will squeeze your cock until you explode inside me.'

They ate and Paris studied the tension between these two women who were addicted to the pleasures of the orgasm. They had within their faces the same broken hunger he had seen in the eyes of heroin addicts, women intent on the one act they felt defined them and which eventually led to their being broken by the pleasure they would ultimately have to forsake for a paler existence, as if by indulging it they lost it.

And Paris thought about his own position in these many dramas he had witnessed and participated in, and he considered that he was always on the edge of others' lives, pandering to the needs of others, then strolling out of the dramas as easily as he entered them, as smoothly as he slid his cock inside the many wet and hungry snatches he encountered on the way.

The manager of the restaurant, Ingrid, was a debauched ancient harlot who watched as the sisters argued and Brigitte showed her cunt to Paris as he ate. She had one hand on the door frame, the other deep inside her dress and from time to time her elbow jerked as she let loose a sigh. When Brigitte went through to pay, the owner said, 'you lucky woman, what I would give for that man's cock inside me.'

As they walked back Brigitte said, 'We eat there often, she sometimes has naked parties, we are the decadent part of Düsseldorf.'

Inside the house Brigitte began to strip as Heidi reached inside Paris's trousers.

'I enjoyed my food but what I wanted all along was this hard prick,' she said.

She began to rub Paris's cock as Brigitte came over and removed his shirt. Heidi pulled down her skirt and Paris unbuttoned her blouse, running his hand across her breasts as Brigitte sucked him. He inserted his finger inside Brigitte as Heidi rubbed herself, then he lay on the sofa as each sister sat on his face. He licked Brigitte's cunt while Heidi sucked his cock then he stuck his tongue deep inside Heidi while Brigitte rubbed him.

Then he said, 'Side by side ladies and I will compare arses, I want to give your snatches a good hard pounding.'

He led them over to the window through which the moonlight fell softly onto their naked skin and the two women placed their hands side by side so that their breasts were almost touching and leant on the window sill, staring out at the hungry voluptuous night. Paris inserted a finger in each of them and played with their clits as they moaned. Their flesh was pink and beyond the window Paris saw a flashing green light somewhere, and it seemed to him that was his life among the garden of pink bodies, green lights allowing him access to women wherever he went.

Brigitte moaned low and deeply, while Heidi moaned in a staccato desperate fashion that told Paris she was about to explode.

'Stick it in me Paris,' Heidi yelled, 'fill my pussy with your cock.'

'Me first, Paris,' Brigitte said, 'look at my cunt, it's dripping.'

Paris thrust his cock inside Brigitte while he continued to rub Heidi. He pounded Brigitte's pussy as her tits knocked against her sister's.

Then he pulled his cock out and, sticking his finger inside Brigitte he entered Heidi from behind. He pushed it deep inside and she screamed, 'Fill me with hot come, Paris, give my cunt all your juice, pump it from your throbbing cock.'

He pushed against Heidi's buttocks, and he fucked her hard and long, eventually exploding and filling her with come.

As Paris stood there with the two naked women across whose bodies the moonlight drifted like a watchful cloud, his cock erect before him, he saw Heidi look at her sister with a glance that told him their jealousy was mounting like a flame, like the flame he rode in Rome, like all the passionate hearts he entered and left. And he wondered where his gigolo's life would lead him.

Brigitte took his cock in her hand.

'My snatch wants more, fill me up, Paris.'

He looked at her cunt, her clit protruding from it, her nipples erect.

Heidi placed her hand over Brigitte's and both women squeezed his cock.

'His cock prefers my cunt,' Heidi said, 'it is tighter than yours, look at my lips, wet and juicy.'

'I will make sure his cock uses up its last inch of erection, and fills me with all his come,' Brigitte said, 'look at my beautiful pussy.'

Paris fucked them both again, he rode these two sexual addicts, and as his cock slid in and out of their dripping clutching snatches he felt the twitching of disaffection with the life he led and the endless pathways of flesh he rode like the eternal city of lust. He knew a rage for arousal dwelt in every town he passed through like some spectre of satyriasis. He existed beneath the hem of polite society like some archetype of the primal erection, physical, absolute, desired and undesiring, a loveless whore cast among the flesh of women everywhere who tired of them as soon as he penetrated them to their sleeping core. For he was the nocturnal lover with a passport to every city's lustful heart that beat rapidly between midnight and the slow dawn that brought memories and guilt to the pulsing orgasms he gave his conquests. He removed conscience from his women for the time he spent inside them. He was the omnipresent seducer who frequented hotels and houses where hidden desires lingered like the perfume on a concubine's skin, he was an impenetrable Lothario who handled the bodies of females in the ubiquitous town of secret desires which they hid by day and which Paris aroused by night. And in that moment he saw his own reflection, he was a nomadic gigolo. He dwelt in the Noir City. For the city was the body of flesh, a map of sex. It was the place of thresholds and sudden yearnings, it was the erogenous zone of collective lust, it was the knot of arteries that threaded through the passion of women everywhere and Paris knew he could not stay, for by staying he lost his allure and his appeal, he was separate, not of society, a forbidden dream. As such he realised that he was the Metropolis of desire. Paris was sex city and all the tourists were women all the buildings places of desire.

All of this occurred to Paris as he shared his cock between the sisters that night. The act he'd performed a thousand times came into a focus so sharp now that he felt on the verge of some psychological orgasm of knowledge, as if his self-awareness was gushing semen inside him.

Brigitte and Heidi lay back on the sofa, their mouths and cunts open and speaking the language of unfettered desire. Paris entered their cunts again, one after another until he gave Brigitte such a violent orgasm that she tore a hole in the sofa with her nails. He was animalising them, and he made sure Heidi experienced the thing he knew she craved. He pumped her snatch until he felt her pussy gush and her scream tore the night and he kept pushing deep inside her until he saw the other Heidi there, the one he'd glimpsed lurking in her glances, and she looked back at him out of her face. He kept pushing until he came inside her, releasing a serpent from his spine, and he watched the light fill the room.

Afterwards he watched the women sleep side by side, spent, exhausted by their jealous fire and sexual hunger. But Paris felt more alive than ever and hungered for a hundred women lined up one by one so that he could pound their dripping cunts. He stood in the room naked, his cock erect. He saw the images of women everywhere lost among ephemeral dreams that he entered like a wraith, and it occurred to him that he existed outside the body of flesh and perhaps he was not aging but recreating himself with each seduction and penetration.

He licked their cunts as they lay there, tasting the come and ecstasy of their lips. He rolled his tongue inside them.

Eventually Paris went upstairs to try to sleep. He lay there and considered how he would tire of these two sisters and he wondered what it was he sought in the idle hours in fuck houses all across Europe. The seductions were easy for him, and he knew he was seeking something else, and it left him alone as dawn broke pink and silent across the sleeping rooftops.

When he rose Brigitte and Heidi were having breakfast. Brigitte sat at the kitchen table wearing a white negligee that was open at the top, while Heidi wore a blue nightie.

Paris poured coffee and ate some bread and plum jam. He got the sense that an argument had taken place between them.

'You can come to the shop today,' Brigitte said.

It was a declaration of her taking control and Paris saw through it to the drama beneath it. He saw through the glances the sisters gave each other to the fierce struggle that had raged between them all their lives, and he knew they used sex to try to maintain a sense of identity in their relationship.

He went to the shop and watched the tired women enter and look in his direction. They came there seeking relief from their unsatisfying lives and Brigitte sold them toys and clothes that made them feel more exciting and desired for a day or so until they needed something else.

He served them, and sometimes was asked for his opinion on how they looked, and he paid them the customary compliments expected from a man by desperate women. They seemed to come there looking for him, as if he was known among the frustrated clientele Brigitte catered to like a madam.

One afternoon when Paris was tending the shop alone, Ingrid entered. She walked over to him and said, 'I wonder what it feels like.'

'What it feels like?' Paris said.

'To have you inside my cunt.'

'I know you run a rather unusual establishment and must have seen some of the nudity the other night when we ate.'

'Nudity?' Ingrid said.

She was wearing a raincoat and she began to undo the buttons. She opened it to show Paris her withered breasts and the black hair that clung to her cunt. Then she took one of the dildos out of the back room and returning, shoved it inside her snatch and began to masturbate in front of Paris.

'Paris would you slide your big cock in here, look at how far the dildo goes in, I can feel myself coming having you watch me frig.'

She pushed deep inside her snatch and began to scream, 'Cock, cunt, sex, ecstasy we are the depraved Düsseldorf whores.'

Then she pulled it out and placed the wet dildo on the counter. She looked at Paris and said, 'I will take your cock inside me and make sure you come, will you come inside my cunt?'

She ran her finger along the dildo's edge.

'I will make you so hard you will want to fill me like a river.'

Just then Heidi came into the shop.

'What do you think you're doing Ingrid?' she said.

Ingrid did up her raincoat and walking up to Heidi said, 'Huh! You're not the only women with wet and hungry snatches round here.'

Then she left the shop.

'I am so sorry,' Heidi said to Paris, 'she is a slut.'

She ran her hand down to Paris's crotch and felt his cock.

'Fill my cunt with it.'

She locked the shop and Paris fucked her in the back room surrounded by the paraphernalia of sexual desperation.

When she left, Paris felt that the clientele he served were freakish and consumed by a lack of fulfilment that made them easy prey for those who pandered to desires. And he thought that he did not want to be one of them, for he was neither a pimp nor a prostitute but a sexual trader seeking a new erotic aesthetic.

He was tiring of the menagerie and of the sisters' demands. And while he might satisfy them, he wanted to satisfy himself. He thought of Brigitte's cunt, set on display as they ate, her lips gaping beneath the food she chewed. He thought of Heidi's jealousy. She spent less time at the shop than her sister, and each evening Paris returned he would find her waiting for him.

Once he entered the bathroom to find her naked there. She pulled him towards her hungrily and he fucked her in the shower.

He fucked both sisters, often in the same room, although they tried to secure his time alone more and more. It was clear their resentments towards each other were growing.

He continued to work in the shop, getting bored of the place and thinking of new cities to ride, as if they were each a woman whose flesh he explored. Then he met Anja.

STEALING ANJA.

ONE AFTERNOON WHEN THE RAIN FELL FROM THE SKY AND Paris was staring out of the shop window he saw a beautiful dark haired woman remove a scarf from her head, shake loose the most luxuriant curls of hair he had ever seen in his life and step over a puddle, then walk towards the shop.

He was standing behind the counter when she entered. Paris pretended to be deep in study of a magazine that displayed the naked forms of buxom women washing. He raised his eyes from the picture of a woman sponging her vagina to the look into the clearest brown eyes. She stood there in a double breasted coat, which she removed as Paris imagined her naked. Beneath it she was wearing a violet satin skirt and blouse and she had a thin waist, large breasts, and long legs.

'Is Brigitte here?' she said.

'She is out, is there anything I can help you with?'

'My husband is having a party and he wants me to get some clothes fitting for the occasion, I normally ask Brigitte's advice for this sort of tiresome affair.'

'I am sure I can help you. What sort of thing are you looking for?'

'My husband wants me to dress up as a maid.'

Paris showed her the outfits the store stocked and then he led her to the changing room. At the end of the counter he could see the mirror that stood above the changing area, hidden behind a partition. He watched as she removed her clothes, and stripped down to her bra and G-string. She had a tight arse and toned body and Paris decided he would have her, and disengage himself from the fighting sisters.

When she came out she said, 'How does it suit me?'

'It suits you well, although I would say it is a little beneath you.'

'You are right, it is beneath me, but I have to play these games for my husband.'

'Do you?'

'Here I am prattling on and I don't even know your name.'

'Paris.'

'Well, Paris you have helped me find what I must wear tonight.'

'You are welcome, Mrs...'

'Anja.'

She went to change. When she came back out she handed Paris the maid's outfit. As he packed it up he said, 'Do you live nearby? It is raining and I can accompany you if you wish, I have an umbrella.'

'How kind of you.'

And so he walked her to her house, a large mansion a few kilometres away in Grafenberg. She talked all the way there, asking Paris how he was enjoying Düsseldorf and what his plans were. At the door he said, 'It seems we have a lot to talk about, would your husband object to you meeting me for a coffee perhaps? I have an interesting proposition to make to you.'

'A proposition? How intriguing,' she said. She bit her lower lip, 'Yes let us have a coffee, come to my house tomorrow, around ten? My husband will be out.'

'I look forward to it.'

'And I look forward to hearing your proposition.'

Paris walked back to the two sisters.

#

At the house he found Brigitte and Heidi arguing.

'I want to spend the evening with Paris,' Heidi said.

'I found him, why should you have him all to yourself?'

'I don't always want to stare at your snatch while I am being filled with his cock.'

'And what makes you think I want to look at yours?'

'Ladies why are you always arguing these days?' Paris said.

'Why do you think?' Brigitte said.

Heidi slumped down in a chair and Paris poured them all a glass of Riesling.

He fucked them both that night, one after the other, and watched them snake around each other, their jealousy palpable in the room as he thought of Anja.

Paris realised that the thrill of seduction was fading from him, the extremities he sought in the bodies of these women were now part of everyday life and as such they had lost their allure and he knew he needed something else, something more. The next day while Brigitte was at the shop and Heidi in the shower, he dressed in his finest suit and made his way to Anja's house, stopping to look in the window of a camera store on the way.

She greeted him wearing a white skirt and blouse and led him though to an ornate living room with plump cushions on the chairs and sofa.

Anja poured them coffee.

'Would you like some cake?' she said.

'Perhaps just the coffee, thank you.'

'Now tell me about your proposition.'

'My proposition is quite simply this. I would like to take your pictures.'

'Oh, are you a photographer?'

'I am and I can see your face on the cover of magazines.'

'Only my face?'

'I will shoot what you show me, what you consider worthy for me to see.'

'And do you think that some of me might be less worthy than the rest?'

'Not at all, Anja.'

'I am teasing you Paris, men like to be teased. I used to be a model and pose nude. I have no qualms about taking off my clothes, I am sure this will come as no surprise to you since you board with Brigitte and Heidi whose sexual proclivities would make most women blush. Not me. My husband would, however disapprove of you shooting me.'

'Is there some way I could persuade him?'

'No. But there is nothing for it. I will rebel against my shackles. After all, he likes to show me off. He had me wearing the maid outfit the other night, every time I bent over I displayed my arse. He likes to show off what he has, so he can fuck me later when his friends have left and feel he owns me. No one owns me Paris, I am free to do as I please and if I want you to take pictures of me then I will pose for you, naked or not.'

'It seems your husband does not fully value you.'

'Have you got some sample pictures to show me?

'I can bring them next time, I had to leave in a bit of a hurry this morning.'

'Oh? Were Brigitte's and Heidi's demands too much for you? I have heard them talk about you.'

'Demands? No not at all, I am somewhat tired of their arguing.'

'You know they have both boasted about your gift. It is the kind of thing many women here would like to enjoy for themselves.'

'My gift, hm well that could mean many things.'

'I think you know what I am referring to.'

'Anja, may I ask where you are from? Your accent is not German.'

'Is this a dodge, Paris? I am Croatian, from Split where there are many beautiful women.'

'And your husband?'

'Oh he's German. And where are you from Paris?'

'Everywhere. London originally.'

'London? Well, when shall we start?'

'Why not later today?'

'It will have to be tomorrow.'

'Same time?'

'Yes, and how do you want me?'

'Just as you are.'

'Oh you don't want me to strip?'

'Is that what I asked?'

'No, not exactly.'

'I will bring some pictures.'

'Oh come now Paris, you don't have to fool me, I know your little ruse and your larger plan and I am all for it. It is not every day I meet a man such as you in this boring life I lead.'

'And what do you think my plan is?'

'To seduce me. You are not a photographer. I don't care though. I have heard all about you, half of Düsseldorf has and we all want to know if it's true.'

'Then I will show you. And forgive me for my less than honest approach but I wanted to take time with you to enjoy your beauty.'

'Do you not normally take time when you seduce a woman?'

'Oh yes.'

Anja stood up.

'Come tomorrow Paris, visit me here tomorrow.'

#

Things were no better back at the house and Paris went to his bedroom where he thought about his life. It seemed to him that he was still a pickpocket with the sexual nature of a thief, but that he had elaborately wrapped this up in the finest plumage and set it on display to lure women to his seducer's web. And now he wanted to steal Anja, he wanted to steal her away from her husband and enjoy her on his own and he wondered for how long. If he inhabited an underworld it was an underworld of sin and desire. Sex ran things deep down and he knew that, he's known it as a boy observing the behaviour of women. He was here in another city with two sexually deranged sisters. Paris knew that female vanity was as deep as an ocean and he was adept at using it to his advantage, for a gigolo always controlled women.

He thought about how Anja had caught him out and he enjoyed it. She represented something new, a challenge of a different kind and he decided to go downstairs and have some wine. But when he entered the living room the atmosphere told him that the enmity between Brigitte and Heidi was growing by the day. They sat at opposite ends of the room ignoring one another and Paris tried to start a conversation but they spoke only to him.

Eventually he tired of them and went out.

#

The next morning he walked to Anja's house. She let him in wearing a long evening dress, a strange choice, he thought, for a woman who knew she was meeting a man who was there to seduce her. She left him in the living room while she went to get some wine and he studied the pictures of her husband. He was a handsome man, not what Paris expected at all. And the proposition of the theft of his wife now became even more appealing to Paris.

Anja came in with a bottle of fine Kerner.

'I see you are looking at Mr Blau,' she said, giggling.

'Yes, something funny?'

'I was laughing at my maid's outfit.'

'The one he made you wear?'

'But he didn't. I made it up to lure you here.'

'I see.'

'I wanted to seduce you Paris, notable seducer.'

'The best seductions always allow the woman to feel she is doing just that.'

'And is that what you are doing, Paris?'

'I think I know how to give a woman like you pleasure.'

Anja laid her hand on his chest and began to unbutton his shirt. She reached inside and ran her hand down his chest to his stomach.

'I want to see if the rumours I have heard for too long now about you are true, can you make me come in ways I have never come before?'

Paris slipped her dress down to her waist and undid her bra. Her breasts were perfectly shaped, with saucer-like nipples, and he began to suck them as Anja undid his fly.

'I want to see this magnificent cock I have heard so much about, half the women in Düsseldorf have bought dildos and imagine being screwed by you. Is it true?'

And she pulled Paris's cock out and rubbed it until it was erect, then she bent and licked it. She took it in her mouth, running her tongue around the end and sucked hard on it.

'My cunt is dripping for your prick.'

She slipped out of her dress. She stood there in a pair of peach coloured cami knickers. Paris could see the shape of her wet lips beneath the silk. He followed her upstairs to the bedroom where she took them off.

'I want my tongue inside your peach,' Paris said.

Anja lay back and Paris parted her thighs and licked the most enticing cunt he had ever seen. He tongued her clit until she grabbed his head and pulled his mouth further onto her pussy which he lapped and licked until she came.

Then Anja sat on his cock.

'It's true,' she said, 'those sisters are lucky to have shared you, but now I want you to myself. My cunt is full with your prick.'

She pushed down on Paris's chest and rode him until she had another orgasm.

Then Paris spread her legs and licked her again, before he entered her and fucked her deeply until he filled her with come.

Afterwards they lay there in the twilight and drank champagne, admiring one another's bodies. And it seemed to Paris that in Anja he had a woman who might represent a bigger challenge than the idle seductions he had feasted on for too long. And the prospect of leaving with her as opposed to leaving her for another city seemed to Paris to be the change he was looking for among all the bodies and desires he catered to. He ran his hand down Anja's body, along her contours, and her thighs, and felt her buttocks as she sighed.

'What would your husband think?'

'I don't want my husband, I want you. He has mistresses, he is rarely here.'

'How do you plan to leave him?'

'I don't think he'll object.'

#

But he did object.

After Paris had left Anja that evening and returned to the squabbling sisters, Mr Blau returned home and demanded sex from his wife. When Anja refused he slapped her and dragged her to the bed where a fight broke out. He was tearing her clothes from her when Anja kicked out and connected with his balls.

Mr Blau crawled across the room gasping.

'You bastard, you tried to rape me!' she said.

'Rape! You're my wife.'

'You're never here.'

'I work.'

'Fucking your mistress.'

'Hah.'

'Well I have a lover and I am leaving you.'

Mr Blau dragged himself to his feet, his face red with fury.

'Lover! No you don't, you little slut, showing your pussy to strangers are you? Well I will show you what your pussy is for, it's for me not for some bastard to fuck while I work to pay the bills, come here and let me show you what I have for you and when I have finished you won't want a lover.'

Anja was screaming as he dragged her by the hair into the bathroom where he turned on the light.

#

Paris was in his bedroom at the house thinking of how he would steal Anja from her husband. The fact that she belonged to another was in itself an aphrodisiac to his seducer's heart, and yet he struggled with the constant notion of himself a thief. The idea of this robbery aroused him like no other and he thought of them wandering Europe together and fucking in different destinations. And he thought of how tight and wet Anja's snatch was and all the ways and places he would fuck her. Then it occurred to him that no theft would be necessary. And he wondered if without theft he might find a permanence he was beginning to desire. He thought of Anja's beautiful body beneath him while downstairs a row broke out.

#

Mr Blau was stripping the clothes from Anja as she struggled on the floor. As he tore her dress from her she reached for a bottle of perfume and brought it down hard on his head. Mr Blau put his hand to his head and staggered about the bathroom as Anja stood up.

'You bitch! Now you'll taste my belt, I am going to scar you and fuck you!'

Anja brought the bottle down on his head again. It splintered and she drove the jagged glass into his skull. Mr Blau collapsed and Anja ran to the bedroom where she sat on the bed with her feet up, clutching the bedclothes. It was dark and she sat there thinking of Paris as Mr Blau came into the room. The Anja raced downstairs to the kitchen.

#

The row was driving Paris to distraction and after an hour he went down to placate the two sisters. Brigitte was screaming at Heidi, who turned round as Paris entered the living room.

'Fuck her Paris, she thinks I have stolen you,' she said.

'Ladies, I think it's time I left Düsseldorf,' Paris said, 'my presence here can only exacerbate a relationship that has already grown sour.'

'I see, you want to leave with her,' Brigitte said.

'No.'

'She is beyond reason,' Heidi said.

'Then explain why I have not had your cock inside me for two nights Paris,' Brigitte said, 'is it because her snatch has had it all?'

Paris turned to leave, tired of them. As he did he heard Brigitte scream, 'Bitch!'

'He hasn't slept with me either,' Heidi said.

'Paris!' Brigitte yelled, 'Come with me to the bedroom now and show me.'

Paris thought of Anja and carried on walking upstairs. He heard insults traded, then an increasing crescendo of shouting.

He decided to pack and after some time returned downstairs where both women saw him with his case in the hallway.

'Where are you going?' Brigitte said.

'You two need to sort your differences out while I stay somewhere else.'

'Where will you stay?' Heidi said.

'There are plenty of hotels here.'

'Will you come back?' Brigitte said.

'Maybe.'

He looked at them both standing there, furious, panicked at his departure and he closed the door behind him.

He walked towards Grafenberg. He had noticed a hotel near Anja's house and he took a room there for the night. It was now the early hours of the morning and Paris lay there thinking of what he would do the next day. He did not want to return to Brigitte and Heidi. He would wait until late morning and go to Anja and propose they leave together.

As Paris slept Brigitte and Heidi continued to fight. Shouting could be heard on the street, and alarmed neighbours peeked out of their windows to find out what the notorious sisters were up to now, speculating perhaps this was some new debauchery they were indulging in. Suddenly the commotion ended with a piercing scream, bringing with it a silence that was welcomed by the other residents nearby.

Inside the house Heidi was standing in the kitchen with her back to the door and her hands on her face. Brigitte had a knife sticking out of her stomach which was dripping with blood. Then she fell forwards and Heidi began to scream.

Heidi was arrested that night after she called an ambulance and her sister was pronounced dead.

#

Paris rose the next morning, ate some breakfast at the hotel, and settled his bill. He waited until 10 o'clock, then walked to Anja's house with a clear idea of what he wanted to say to her. He rang the bell. After some minutes Anja opened the door covered in blood.

'I have killed him,' she said.

Paris entered the hall.

'I have been sitting on the sofa wondering if he would stir,' Anja said. 'He is lying there in a pool of blood, and when dawn broke and he didn't move I knew.'

'Stay here.'

Paris went into the living room and inspected Mr Blau's body. He had a kitchen knife buried in his chest and lay facing the ceiling.

Paris poured a glass of brandy and took it to Anja.

'He tried to rape me. He said he would scar me because I told him I wanted to leave and I have found a lover.'

'Well you can't stay here now. The police will arrest you.'

'I have no claim to his house or money, he made sure of that. You won't leave me now Paris, will you?'

'Of course I won't, I want you Anja, and now there is no husband in the way we are free to go wherever we want, but you must get out of here. Drink that and then pack.'

Anja sipped the brandy staring into Paris's eyes, then she went upstairs. He followed her and watched her gather her clothes and a few items of jewellery and place them in a suitcase, then look around her house. She wandered from room to room, avoiding the living room where her husband lay.

'I know you are finding it hard to leave, but you will be sent to prison if they catch you.'

'Won't they find me wherever we go?'

'I know ways of disappearing.'

'I want to be with you, Paris.'

'Then leave here now, take whatever you can, and let us go to the airport.'

Anja gathered a few more things and crammed them into her overflowing case.

'Let's go to Croatia,' she said, 'you will like it there.'

They left the house. As they travelled to Düsseldorf airport in a taxi they saw police cars speeding towards the area where Brigitte and Heidi lived. Anja shuddered.

'I may have only narrowly escaped,' she said.

'How would they know?'

Paris thought about the desire for extremes that had brought him to Düsseldorf and how quickly he had tired of them and of the two warring sisters. He looked at Anja who sat next to him and he felt this was a new beginning for him, and he may have a future with permanence. And it seemed to him that was the thing he lacked from his childhood and during his endless quests for women who would erase the memory of the one before. And this time he did not want erasure but something else.

As Paris and Anja sat in the taxi Heidi was led away by police officers. She said nothing in the car nor at the station, as if the loss of her sister had brought about some loss within herself that removed her identity.

When Paris and Anja got to the airport they found that they had missed the flights to Croatia for that day and so they booked two tickets for the next morning and went to a nearby hotel for the night. Anja did not want to leave the room for fear of the police and so they ordered some food and wine to be sent up.

'They will only be looking for you when your husband's body is discovered, and by then we will be safe,' Paris said.

'The cleaner will come tomorrow afternoon, she will call the police.'

'Once we arrive in your country I will find a way to change your identity quickly.'

'How, Paris?'

'I have visited many cities and there are things they all share, things you can buy in all of them. We can pay someone to give you a new identity.'

'I have taken the money from the safe, we have enough to rent a place for a year or more.'

They ate and afterwards Anja stripped and went over to Paris. She reached inside his trousers, pulled out his cock hungrily, and sucked it. Then he fucked her long and slowly on the hotel bed. Anja wrapped her legs around him and pulled Paris deep inside her. She came as Paris filled her pussy with come, and then they slept. Paris looked at her as she closed her eyes. She looked beautiful and with an innocence that he found appealing. But how could that be, he wondered. She was an artful manipulator, so it seemed unlikely she was innocent.

The next morning they rose early, showered together and had breakfast in their room. Then they went to the airport and caught their plane.

'I think you are going to like Split,' Anja said as they flew out of Germany.

'I already do Anja,' Paris said.

What he meant was the city, the city he recreated wherever he went, and for a brief moment he thought about settling down. Then he realised that the idea was appealing because it was so strange to him, like another country with foreign customs. Anja did attract him, it was true but for how long, he wondered. Paris began to form an idea in his mind of what he would do next in his sexual adventures, for his life was after all an erotic picaresque of mystical proportions, and the need for new women with newer desires did not abate in him even with Anja in his life. He would give her pleasure in her country while he brought his erotic city to it. He would study the women there. He would show them the wildest ecstasies a man can give to a woman. Paris had it clear in his head by the time they landed, he was prepared for a major move in a new direction, stepping from the plane with Eros in his eyes. He was a man with a mission, a gigolo who could have any woman. He was about to show the world that he was great, a sexual anarchist who would start an erotic revolution.